CW01636858

HALLOWEEN IN BRANDEN BAY

KELLY MASON

LITTLE ORCHARD PRESS

Copyright © 2022 by Kelly Mason

All rights reserved.

No part of this book may be reproduced in any form or by any electronic or mechanical means, including information storage and retrieval systems, without written permission from the author, except for the use of brief quotations in a book review.

Cover Design by www.getcovers.com

This is a work of fiction. Names, characters, places and incidents are the product of the author's imagination or are used fictitiously, and any resemblance to actual persons living, or dead, business establishments, events or locales is entirely coincidental.

These books were written in the UK and edited in British English, where some spelling, grammar and word usage will be different to US English.

Created with Vellum

For Callie, Claire and Jennie.

CHAPTER 1

I placed another pumpkin shaped ball of marzipan on top of the frosted carrot cake, then carried it from my kitchen into the seating area of Connie's Café. The café was situated in a large room at the front of the huge Victorian house, that I inherited from my grandma.

"That looks scrummylicious," Lynn said as she made space for the cake.

"If there's something I love, it's a theme," I said as I placed it on the counter.

Lynn ran a spiritualist church, which backed onto my garden and worked part-time in the café. She was in her mid-fifties with shoulder length sliver-blonde hair. She also helped me cope with my newfound gift for seeing the dead.

My regular first customer of the day breezed in.

"It's freezing out there." Annie popped in on her

way to work every morning. She worked as a manager at the funfair and pier. Not only was she my regular customer, she was also one of my best friends. "I'm looking forward to my trip to Martinique to see my aunties. I need a good dose of sun."

"I wish I was coming," I said.

"Well, you can if you like?"

"I might have taken you up on the offer, if I wasn't expecting my parents in December."

Annie undid her jacket and looked around the room. "I'm loving it in here." She approached the counter and beamed. "It looks amazing."

"I do love Halloween," I said.

"The spider bunting is kind of creepy, though." Annie visibly shuddered as she pointed to the wall.

Lynn nodded. "And the fake cobwebs around the pictures look really effective."

"I think hanging the pictures at an angle gives the room a haunted house feel," I said.

"Your place always has a haunted house feel," Annie said with a laugh.

My cat meowed as she sashayed over.

Annie knelt and stroked her ginger fur. "Constance, you look amazing too." My cat was a stray that I'd taken in and named after my grandma, as she reminded me of her, with her bushy hair and green eyes.

Constance gave a low and grumpy meow. I'd wrapped purple and black ribbon around her collar, and she was far from pleased. I would have changed her collar for something spooky, but it was a robust collar, with a GPS tracker as my cat had been abducted in the past and I liked to know where she was at all times.

Annie picked Constance up, while nodding at me. "And you look great as a witch, it suits you."

I put my hand up to the purple pointed hat I was wearing. "I'm hoping that by going all out this week, I might improve the takings."

Lynn heated up milk at my professional coffee machine for Annie's latte.

"Although, I'm a touch nervous," I added. "I've never done Halloween, as a fully-fledged medium." After six months of paranormal sightings, it was becoming less frightening, but I still felt uneasy receiving contact from the other side.

"Do you think you're going to see a lot of spirits?" Annie asked with her brown eyes wide open.

Constance meowed, jumped to the floor and rubbed up against my legs. My cat also reacted to spirits when they were close by.

"I hope not," I said with a shudder.

Lynn shook her head as she handed Annie her latte in a take-out cup. "Halloween is like any other day, as far as spirits are concerned. It's just a festival for regular folk."

"That's a blessing," I said with relief.

Lynn was an experienced medium and had seen

spirits her whole life. "But I'm all in for the candy and themed cake." She sat down, picked up her knitting needles and a ball of bright orange wool.

"I hope you get a lot more people coming in this week with the ghostly theme," Annie said.

"I would have stayed open late this Saturday for the trick-or-treaters, but we have the Halloween Ball at Branden Bay Castle." I wasn't too chuffed about the location of the event. Halloween or no Halloween, that castle was full of spooks.

"I can't wait," Annie said. "I've not been to a ball before." She took a sip of her coffee.

I raised my eyebrows. "We invited you to the Summer Ball with us, but you said it wasn't your scene."

"A girl can change her mind, can't she?" She gave me a coy smile.

"Especially when there's a tall, ripped and gorgeous guy taking her." I laughed.

"Wes says he loves the thought of us dressing up together."

"I bet he does," I said.

For the past couple of months, Annie had been loved up with a croupier we'd met in Bristol while snooping around the casino, as part of an investigation into the murder of a betting shop owner. I had to admit, Wes was easy on the eye. He looked like the kind of guy you'd see on the front cover of a men's health magazine. He was smitten with Annie and had been over to Branden Bay many times since.

"What are you dressing up as?" Annie asked.

"Nothing original," I said. "I'm sticking with the witch look. And you?"

"We're zombies. Wes's younger sister is doing our make-up. We've matching outfits."

"How sweet," I said wondering whether I should have gone matchy-matchy with my boyfriend, H.

"What's H going as?" Lynn asked me.

"He said he's wearing his 'Phantom of the Opera' outfit, as he's too tied up with work to shop for anything new. If he makes it, that is."

"Of course, he'll make it," Annie said. She'd been friends with H since their college days, long before I moved to town. "I'd better get to work." Annie waved as she left. "See you."

I watched her leave the café and cross the road to the promenade, which lined the sandy beach. The sea was charging in with white ripples on top of the waves and Annie's coat flapped around her. Other than one man walking his dog, the beach was empty. Branden Bay in late autumn was like a ghost town compared to the busy, bustling tourist magnet it was in the summer.

"I'll go out the back, I have a batch of sausage rolls to bake," I said with a sigh, wondering how I was going to balance the books over the coming months. *Maybe I should close?* I thought. I was living off savings and far from being a source of income, the café was a drain on my finances.

In the kitchen, I placed the sausage rolls, which I had already prepared, into the oven and set a timer. I leaned on the worktop and looked at a photo I had pinned to the wall of me and my boyfriend, looking into each other's eyes and laughing at a party I'd held. For just over two months, I'd been in a long-distance relationship with Detective Sergeant Blake, although everyone called him H, apart from his mother who still used the name shown on his birth certificate – Henry. I wished he didn't live in the next county. He'd taken a transfer out of town, to Devon, because whenever there was a murder in Branden Bay, it appeared that the spirit of the deceased came to me for help. I often found myself in the thick of the action and treading on the toes of the police. H had been pulled off the juiciest of cases by his officers in command, because of his connection to me, as I had ended up on their suspect list a couple of times. H said that his relationship with me affected his career, and that the town wasn't big enough for the both of us. But there was no denying it, whenever he motored up to Branden Bay on his days off, we had an amazing time.

I moved forward and touched our photograph. I was head over heels in love with him, but had not seen him for three weeks, as he was caught up in a murder investigation involving the Mayor of Exeter and he couldn't get away. I just hoped I wouldn't be going to the Halloween Ball alone, because my friends were already going in pairs.

"Becky."

I jumped as Lynn brought me out of my daydream.

She stood in the kitchen doorway. "You've got a visitor."

"Who?" I asked, hoping it was a surprise visit from H.

"It's Connor Davies."

I gave a quiet groan.

"Shall I tell him you're busy?" Lynn whispered.

Connor Davies was a well-known-to-the-police hard man who owned the casino in Bristol, that Annie's boyfriend worked at. He had taken a shine to me and wasn't taking no for an answer. Connor had made it clear, he wanted to be an awful lot more to me than my friend, and I'd had to lay it out there a couple of times – I was seeing H and not interested. Connor always acted as if I was the most desirable woman on the planet.

"I'll come out and see him," I said washing my hands under the tap. "He'll only come back if I don't." I wiped my hands dry and adjusted my witch's hat, wishing that I'd been given the gift of magic, rather than a psychic one. If I had, I would have cast a spell on Connor to leave me alone.

I entered the café with a friendly grin on my face to find white-blond Connor smiling back at me. He wore a white suit with a crisp white shirt and an electric blue tie.

"Becky, you look beautiful," he said. "Now I know why I feel you've put a spell on my heart." His ice-blue eyes widened.

Connor was holding my cat in his arms. Luckily her paws were clean. He stroked the top of Constance's head.

Now, my cat is one of two things – affectionate, purring, rubbing up against you, or hissing and snarling, dishing out skin busting swipes. But she stared at me, with a blank expression, as if she'd just got back from the taxidermist. And this reflected the way I saw Connor Davies. I didn't hate him, but as lovely and charming as he was to me personally, I couldn't relax in his presence. I didn't trust him.

"Can I get you a coffee?" I asked in a breezy voice.

"Americano. Black."

"I got it," Lynn called from the counter.

"I have a proposal for you, Becky," Connor said, stroking my cat like a villain out of a Bond movie. Indeed, if he'd auditioned for a part in the action film franchise, I was convinced he'd have got it. I guess fear was splashed all over my face, as after a short pause, he threw his head back and laughed. "Not a marriage proposal, a business proposal."

No way, I thought. I wasn't about to get involved with any dirty money.

"Sit down, Becky. I'm serious."

I gestured towards a window table, from where I could see Connor's white limousine parked. Passing customers were more likely to come in if they saw us in seats. We sat down as Connor held onto Constance. She inched her paw across the table towards me, as if to say she was desperate to move onto my lap, but Connor lifted her paw and began to slowly massage it. My cat's eyes opened even wider.

"What did you have in mind?" I said returning my gaze to Connor.

"As you know, I bought all of the betting shops owned by the late Eddie Fly, and one of those is situated in Branden Bay High Street."

I nodded. "But you can't open it because Branden Bay Council won't approve a gambling venue."

"Exactly. I've spoken to the Councillors, and they're not up for it. It doesn't seem the right time to sell property in the current economic climate, so I've decided to open a charity shop instead." He sat back with Constance still in his arms and smiled at me with a satisfied grin, as if waiting for me to shower him with praise for his charitable nature. It seemed that maybe he was turning a new leaf. But the cynic in me thought, *money laundering racket.*

"I want you and Constance to be the faces of the charity."

Constance slowly turned her head to look at him.

Lynn came over and placed drinks in front of us. "What a marvellous idea."

"Thank you," he said to her, then turned back to me. "It's going to be called *Cat Lovers.* Most of the shop will be for second-hand goods and a small selection of new goods, which will be cat related stock. The profits will be divided between our favourite cat charities." He smiled at me as Lynn moved away and busied herself.

I stared at him, wondering what it was really all about.

"I've been blessed in life, and I think it's time I gave back, don't you?" He touched the scar running across his cheek. He was an attractive man, if you get a kick out of the dangerous gangster type.

"When's it opening?" I asked as I flushed red, wracking my brain for an excuse not to be involved with this charity, as amazing as it sounded.

"I've instructed my fitters and am planning to open at the end of November."

"Where are you sourcing your goods?" I asked.

"Tara said she'd ask around locally." Connor's sister, Tara was a gym instructor who had recently opened a business in Branden Bay. "Do you have anything you can donate?" he asked me.

"Actually, yes," I said. "I sold the large antiques I inherited from my grandma at auction this summer, but I've a few things cluttering up my attic room." At least I could donate to the charity shop, even if I didn't get involved.

Constance gave a grumpy meow.

"I can come up now and take a look at them, if you like?" he said with a small smile.

There was no way I wanted Connor Davies climbing the stairs to my bedrooms. "I need to get back to serving," I said, looking around the empty café.

"Are you having business troubles with a lack of visitors?" he asked.

"I've certainly noticed a drop in footfall since autumn arrived," I said. "But we often get the odd visitor at this time of day."

As I said it, the café door opened and, my other regular customer, Mrs Jessup, came in. She was my next-door neighbour and loved to chat with Lynn and spend an hour reading her books. I stood up, signalling to Connor that I was done talking to him.

"So you're in?" he asked as Constance wriggled free and jumped to the floor before giving another low meow.

"I'll think about it," I said.

Connor drank some of his Americano then rose from his chair. "I'm staying up at Millar's this evening as I'm visiting Tara today. I'll pop in tomorrow to hear your decision. Unless you fancy meeting me later this evening for a meal?"

Millar's was a swanky hotel at the end of the prom, in an elevated position. The hotel was well known for its fancy food and impeccable service with a bar that boasted beautiful views across the bay. But I didn't fancy spending the evening with Connor Davies.

"Sorry, I'm off to a friend's place for dinner." I gave a nervous laugh.

"I know, the policeman wouldn't like it." He took a few more sips from his coffee, then called out his thanks to Lynn and left.

As I watched him get into his white limo, Constance wailed, and I started to think of excuses for why I could not go into the charity business with him. I didn't need to be psychic to know that it would be a bad move.

CHAPTER 2

"I think it's a great idea," Annie said as she brought a pot of sweet potato curry to her dining table. We were eating a meal at her flat which was on the top story of a converted house, with our mutual friend Izzy, a super model turned newspaper reporter.

"But Connor Davies?" I said. "Everyone knows he's dodgy."

"Wes reckons he's not as bad as people say," Annie continued. "He loves working for him."

"Conner is a crime lord, watched by the police," I said with a shake of my head.

"Darling, has he ever been charged?" Izzy asked me as she raised her eyebrows.

"Well, no. But H said he's a slippery character."

"You've made it quite clear to Connor that you're not interested in romance, so there's no problem there," Annie added. "And I know he's always flirting with you but Wes says he flirts with every pretty woman that steps foot in the casino and has a lot of girlfriends. He has a flirtatious manner. Some people are just like that. I mean, look at Izzy," she said gesturing at our mutual friend.

"And what's that supposed to mean?" Izzy said sitting back in her chair.

"You'd flirt with a lettuce," Annie said.

She's got a point," I said with a laugh as I spooned curry onto my plate.

"Utterly untrue," Izzy said running a hand over her blonde bob.

"Come off it, you bat your eyelashes at everyone," Annie added.

Izzy gave a long sigh. "I can't help it if I have so many fans."

"You even flirt with Constance," I said.

My cat raised her head and meowed as if in agreement.

"Maybe a little," Izzy said helping herself to fluffy white rice. "But less about me, Connor must know you're off limits romantically, sweetie. After all, you're dating a policeman."

"Am I?" I sighed as I put salad onto my plate, made with rocket, sweetcorn, bell peppers and fresh chillies. "He's not here, is he?"

Annie passed me a flatbread. "H said he's catching

up on paperwork now, so he can be in Branden Bay for the weekend."

Annie, Izzy, and H had been friends since college and met once a month at each other's places for dinner. When I moved to Branden Bay, they'd included me in their regular get-togethers, and H was notably missing.

"Darling, he adores you," Izzy said. "I think you should do the charity shop with Connor. You're well known around town and just think about the poor little kitties that need your help."

Constance meowed, although I wasn't so sure it was in agreement.

I frowned. "I've got the café to look after."

"You said it's dead in the winter."

"I still have my regulars to think of," I said.

"And you said he asked you to be the face of the shop. He doesn't expect you to work there," Izzy said. "Sweetie, it's like you'll be part of the brand. It'll be great for your image. I've partaken in brand awareness for charities before. It's so rewarding."

"I didn't think you liked Connor?" I said.

"True," Izzy said. "I don't approve of the way he uses scantily dressed women in his V.I.P. bar. But ..." she fluttered her eyelashes.

"Izzy?" I said in a slow voice. I could see her mind whirring before my eyes.

She sighed. "Okay. If I'm honest, I've nothing to

write about this week. A piece on you and the opening of a charity shop in Branden Bay would be fab. Whenever there's a photo of Becky James, The Medium of Branden Bay and Constance her psychic cat, on the front page of The Gazette, the papers fly out." Izzy had reported on all of the spooky cases I had solved and had even sold one of the stories to a national newspaper.

Annie laughed. "Come on you two, eat. The food is getting cold."

I thought about Connor Davies as we ate the delicious meal. I didn't want him popping into the café the following day. So, after we'd eaten a rum soaked sponge with coconut ice-cream, I texted him to say that I wanted to hear more about the charity project and arranged to meet him at the shop. I also mentioned that Izzy would be joining us.

IT WAS A BRIGHT MORNING, with a frosty sea breeze, but a sunny day that lifted my spirits, as Izzy and I walked the short distance from my house to the High Street. I'd left Lynn knitting in the café, which was empty when we'd left. Constance poked her head out of my bag and her fluffy hair ruffled in the wind. She liked to follow me around everywhere and had a habit of jumping into one of the tote bags I'd inherited from Grandma, whenever I left the house. People were now used to seeing us together.

We turned into the traditional Victorian High

Street, with shops built in stone, mined from the local quarry, with many having a bay window as the facade. Most of the businesses were the type you'd expect to find in a seaside resort. Cafés and shops with beach paraphernalia, which in the summer months had brightly coloured displays of buckets, spades and nets, set on the pavements. Also on the High Street was Corelli's, my favourite Italian restaurant, a bank, a pet shop, the job centre and an antique store.

As we got closer to Connor's shop, I heard the rumble of his limo as he drew up.

Connor's driver opened the door for him.

"Isabella," Connor said as he stepped out of the limo. "Thanks for agreeing to come. It's great to have you covering the project."

I had to hand it to him — Connor was smooth. And as he led us into the shop, Izzy lapped it up, gliding into the room like a swan. Her tall frame and grace gave away her previous career. They chatted away, massaging each other's egos as hard as I'd knead a slab of bread dough.

After wandering around the shop space with Connor as he explained his plans, I held Constance in my arms and looked out to the street. Opposite was a café, the sort where you would buy a full English fry up, unlike the bakery style sandwiches and cake I served up at my place. A man sat in the window, staring at me. He noticed me clock him and went back to his meal. I felt a nip of static in my neck and Constance growled.

I turned back as Connor changed the conversation to the shop.

"I'll be advertising in the Gazette for local volunteers."

"I can arrange that for you and the article will be free advertising, of course," Izzy said.

"Thank you." Connor flashed a smile and gestured to the left of the room. "I've spoken to the cat rescue charity that I donate to, and they will have a display stand over there. I wish you could see my cats, Becky. Maybe one day you'll visit my home? They would love you."

I'd heard from Tara, that Connor was much nicer to his cats than he was to human beings.

I changed the subject, not wanting to firm up a home visit with Connor. "Where are you going to source your new goods? We don't want to upset the pet shop up the road."

"Great point. But as a charity shop, we're only permitted to sell a small percentage of new gear. I was thinking more of novelty items, than pet supplies."

"I'll have a word with them," I said. "I think maybe if they have leaflets for their own shop, you could put them on the counter and promote them, so they know this place is not a threat."

"You're very thoughtful, Becky. That's why I'm pleased to have you on board."

What? I thought, I hadn't actually said *yes*. "Well, I'd like to think about – "

Izzy interrupted. "I think we should take your picture outside the shop and go for the angle of bringing more life to the High Street. Providing somewhere for people to pick up a bargain and help destitute kitties. And I'll run the story of how Becky rescued poor Constance."

"I agree," Connor said.

"And then for the opening," Izzy continued. "We can do a complete spread. Come along my darlings. I'll take some shots now."

Connor stroked Constance's head as I held her, then took my arm leading me towards the door. As we walked onto the pavement, I realised I'd somehow agreed to the venture, hoping very much it wasn't a cover for one of Connor's shady operations.

Izzy held her smartphone. "I'll take these myself and then bring the photographer here for the grand opening."

Once outside, I posed with Connor and frowned as Izzy asked us to move closer together. At least Constance was between us. The guy I'd seen in the café opposite watched on, and he too lifted his phone as if he was taking a picture. I would have mentioned it to Connor, but as he had a reputation for making people disappear, I wasn't quite sure what he would do if he thought someone was spying on us. I realised that the guy in the café might just be nosey, so I kept it to myself. After all, in Branden Bay I was famous and Izzy even more so. But as we said goodbye to Connor, I saw the guy scuttle down the street and felt a stronger buzz in the nape of my neck. Static in my body was either a sign that there was a spirit in the vicinity or that danger was in the air. And as ghosts don't usually carry mobile phones, I guessed it was danger. I began to regret any connection I had to Connor Davies.

CHAPTER 3

"I don't believe it," I shouted at my reflection in the dressing table mirror, situated in my bedroom, at the back of the house.

Constance wailed and jumped off the bed – I had clearly startled her.

I took a deep breath and looked out of the window at my garden, which was only just visible in the twilight. I had gazed out at that view over many years, since it had been the bedroom I slept in when I'd visited Grandma as a child, during every school holiday.

Jeff burst into the room. "Have you seen a spirit?" He was one of my two lodgers and a paranormal investigator I had met during my first case.

"What's up?" He pressed me for an answer.

We were joined by my other lodger, Dannie, who I had taken in after she'd lost her day job, which was partly my fault, as I'd named her as a suspect in my second case. She of course was innocent, and I'd taken her in out of sympathy. She was now learning book-keeping up at Branden Bay Technical College and helped me out with my accounts and admin for the café.

I looked from one to the other, both were twenty-one and six years younger than me. Jeff was dressed in a khaki boiler-suit, channelling the ghost-catcher look, and Dannie was dressed as a ghost and wore swathes of white voile, which looked suspiciously like the nets from my spare room window. Her long blonde hair was loose and complimented her outfit.

We were all set for the Halloween Ball, although were not going together. Jeff was taking his new girl-friend, Iona. Yep, it was his first girlfriend, a receptionist from the Budget Inn who had taken a shine to him after joining a couple of his ghost hunts. Dannie was going with her friend, Blue, named that way by her friends, after her indigo-coloured hair.

Dannie put her hands on her hips. "Come on then, what's wrong? Please don't tell me we've another ghost in here? I'm not sure I can cope with that, again."

"Have you seen a Halloween apparition?" Jeff asked, his eyes darting around the place as he lifted his phone and scanned the room with a ghost-hunting app.

I shook my head and lifted my mobile phone. "H has blown me out. And he texted! He didn't even call."

Constance jumped onto my lap and I felt instantly calmed as I stroked her soft fur.

Dannie's expression softened, and she came over and put a hand on my shoulder. "I'm sorry. Do you want to go up with me and Blue?"

"I won't bother. I can stay here with Constance. I don't want to leave her anyway, in case of any mischievous trick-or-treaters."

"Boss, you've got to go. The whole gang will be there, even Lynn's coming," Jeff said.

"So why can't he make it?" Dannie asked.

"He said there's been a development on the murdered mayor case." I looked down at the phone and the quick text I had fired back at him which said:

It's not working. I can't do this.

Tears smarted my eyes and Constance nuzzled my hand. I decided to recall and delete the text as I'd been a bit hasty. But the phone notified me that the message had already been read. I turned my phone off and placed it face down on the dresser. *It's true,* I thought. *Long-distance relationships don't work.*

"You can't stay here all on your own at Halloween?" Jeff said exasperated, as if I was just about to miss Christmas Day.

I sighed. "Okay, I'll see you up there." I turned back to the mirror. "But I won't be ready for a while, I haven't done my witches make-up yet."

"You're not going to bail out, are you?" Dannie asked.

"I'll be there. I promise," I said, then regretted it immediately, knowing I wouldn't be able to back out.

CONSTANCE WATCHED from the café French windows as I waited outside. Whilst we went most places together, the Halloween Ball with thumping music and hundreds of guests was too busy for her, even if security did agree to let her in. I stood at the front gate, having called a taxi. Izzy was my go-to plus-one, but she was going with her new friend, Martha, an artist I had yet to meet. And Lynn was going up with her friend from the weekly bridge club she attended.

Typically, the cab didn't show. I sighed as I pulled the front gate to and started the twenty minute walk up to the castle. I stormed along the road wearing my Doc Martin boots, black and purple striped tights, and a black tutu with a long-sleeved lace top. As witches go, I guess I was a pretty sassy one. I had crimped my red hair, which was blowing around in the sea breeze and I carried my pointed purple hat, which would have blown away in the wind if I'd worn it. I didn't fancy chasing it along the prom.

After dodging a few trick-or-treaters, I stopped halfway up the hill as the party venue came into sight. The building usually glowed a soft yellow hue, but there were lights projecting purple onto the castle with images of ghosts flying across the walls. Millar's hotel hired the castle for events, and they had done a pretty good job with the spooky decoration.

I still had another three hundred yards to go when a car slowed and drove alongside me. I heard the window being lowered and looked to my right.

"Becky. Is that you?"

I turned to see a vampire smiling at me. It was Connor Davies. "Oh, hi," I said with an inward sigh.

"I'm sure you said you had a date?" he said.

"He's busy," I said.

"Step inside." He gestured with a wide smile that revealed his fangs.

I laughed. "I've already walked half a mile uphill. I'm sure I can do the last stretch.

He pushed open the door of his white limo. "It's a steep gradient. Get in and save your legs for the dance floor."

I shrugged, walked over and got in.

The limo was nice, not as sleek as the type Izzy liked to travel around in, it was a Hummer, a much beefier ride.

"I didn't expect you to travel alone," Connor said. He looked even more menacing in his vampire outfit, which was white with an electric blue cravat and was a perfect fit, I guessed with his rumoured millions he could afford a bespoke outfit.

"I'm not the only person without a date, by the looks of it?"

"Unfortunately, my romantic life is complicated."

“I bet it is,” I said with a grin, remembering what Annie had mentioned about his various girlfriends. I gestured to his clothes. “The outfit suits you.” He really could be a model from the front cover of a novel. Maybe a vampire mafia romance.

“It will be an honour to walk in with the famous Becky James.” He opened his eyes wide. “You look ... tempting.” He bared his vampire teeth.

I laughed. Connor was a bit over the top, but he did make me smile. He was quite funny with a wicked sense of humour, after you got over the fear that he might actually kill you.

The car stopped. The driver came around, opened the door and helped me out.

Connor and I stood at the foot of the castle steps. Looking up, I felt a painful burst of static travel from the base of my spine, right up to the top of my head and shuddered.

“Are you okay?” Connor asked. “Have you picked up the presence of a paranormal being?”

“It’s to be expected in a place this old. Jeff comes up here on regular ghost hunts and says there’s a lot of activity.”

“Ah yes, Jeff. I’ve read all about him in Isabella’s articles. I must join one of those hunts. Maybe we could go together?”

“It’s not my idea of fun,” I said, wanting to about turn and go home. Looking to the entrance, I had to admit, the decorations looked even better close-up.

Lanterns lit the path with carved pumpkins dotted around the lawns.

"Let's make our entrance," Connor said as the Hummer rumbled away.

As we climbed the steps, we didn't exactly match as a couple. We looked odd, but as much as I'd wanted to be ascending the steps with H, I felt better not going in alone. I planned to find my friends as soon as we got inside.

We went through the large entrance doors, passed the cloak room and showed our tickets to the security guard. As we entered the main party room, the music thumped so loudly it vibrated in my chest.

"Connor." Tara approached us dressed much sexier than me, with a long Morticia style dress with a split, revealing a long and toned leg. Her career as a gym instructor was definitely being showcased. She usually had her hair tied up in a high ponytail but was wearing a black wig that cascaded over her shoulders.

"Becky." I turned to find Marcus, my ex- boyfriend. He was dressed in a black suit, presumably as Gomez. We'd split up when I'd moved from London to Branden Bay. However, he had come to the town in the summer, chasing a client and had decided to stay. It still felt slightly weird having him living in my new town, but there was no animosity left between us and no romance either. We had both moved on.

"Where's H?" Marcus asked me, as Connor chatted to Tara.

“Stuck on a case,” I said.

“So, you came with Connor?” His eyes widened.

“No, we just arrived at the same time. How’s it going with Tara?” Marcus and Tara were lodging in H’s house while he was away. Although there was no official romance, I could tell Marcus had eyes for Connor’s sister.

“It’s just a friendship, really.”

“But you’re working on it?”

“She’s out of my league. But business is going great. I picked up another client this week.” Marcus was a marketing consultant.

“Let’s get into the party. I’m dying to see everyone’s outfits," I said.

Once we went through the doors, I slipped away to look for my friends. The room was a mass of black, purple, orange and red outfits. It would have been so nice to be here with H. *Some things are not meant to be*, I thought. I’d left my phone at home. I didn’t want to see a text from him, in case it said – *You’re right, let’s call it a day*.

I decided to deal with my broken relationship in the morning.

I spotted Izzy. She was dressed as a bride – a very elaborate bride I might add, with swathes of netting and very white makeup with a stark red vampire bite on her neck. I approached her.

She waved as she saw me. “Becky, darling, you’re here.” She looked around. “Where’s H?”

I shrugged. “He can’t make it.”

“Oh, sweetie. I know he was looking forward to it. He’ll be devastated.”

I felt slightly bad about the text I’d sent him. “I don’t think it’s going to work, Izzy,” I shouted above the music.

“Nonsense. You two are meant to be.” She looked around. “Martha!” She waved to a vampire who approached us. Izzy placed a hand on Martha’s arm. “Meet Becky James, the Medium of Branden Bay.”

“Hello,” Martha said, baring her fangs in an awkward grin as if she was worried they would fall out.

“Nice to meet you,” I smiled at the dark-haired woman dressed in a black suit with a red-lined cape. “I hear you’re an artist?”

She nodded. “I met Izzy at an exhibition in Paris.” She removed her fangs which were coming out as she spoke. “Then we bumped into each other in London a couple of weeks ago. She’s so encouraging.”

“You’re an amazingly talent, darling.” Izzy patted Martha’s arm.

I knew that Izzy had commissioned Martha to paint her portrait. But was waiting for the right time, creatively to paint it.

“So, you had to walk in alone?” Izzy asked me.

“No, Connor arrived at the same time, so we came in together.”

As if by magic, he appeared by my side. “Isabella.” He smiled at Izzy. “How’s the article going?”

"It'll be in this coming issue." It was a weekly paper which hit the shops every Thursday. "Although the piece will be online sooner than that."

I noticed Martha scowl at Connor. I'm sure she didn't usually look so menacing, but dressed as Dracula, she looked as if she was going to take a chunk out of his neck. A vision of airborne duelling vampires appeared before my eyes, one dressed in black, the other in white, with their capes flapping behind them.

"Would you like to dance?" Connor asked me.

"I'm looking for my friends," I said.

He stuck his arm out. "Let me escort you." I decided to go with him because, clearly, Martha was not a Connor fan.

"See you later, Izzy," I waved. "Nice meeting you Martha."

"You take care, sweetie," Izzy said as Martha continued to scowl at Connor.

We'd travelled about ten yards when someone called his name.

"Mr Davies." It was a woman, maybe in her thirties. It was difficult to tell with the feline mask, but she was clad in a black P.V.C cat suit, showing off a very fit physique. She topped the look with a pair of black cat ears.

That must be hot to wear, I thought, hoping she didn't have to make too many visits to the bathroom.

"Helen," Connor replied.

"Who's your little friend?" she said, eying me up and down having emphasised the 'little'.

Okay, so I'm not much more than five feet, but I just wished people didn't keep going on about it. I hadn't helped myself by wearing flats, when everyone else seemed to be in heels.

"It's the famous, Becky James, The Medium of Branden Bay," Connor said.

I could tell by her reaction, she wasn't impressed.

"I won't keep you," Connor said, and steered me away. "That's my wife, Helen."

I stopped in my tracks. "Your wife?"

He chuckled, which was a bit disconcerting, with him dressed the way he was. "Ex-wife, hopefully soon to be official. We split two years ago, but the financial separation has been intense. I made her a reasonable offer. Why should the wife get half when she was never involved in my business? She always kept out of my activities."

Wise woman, I thought. I didn't blame her, seeing as Connor was supposedly a crook.

"She needs to get a job and to stop sapping the life out of me. No wonder she's still single."

I looked over my shoulder as Helen Davies stared after us, that was one pussy cat that was not purring.

"Connor!" A young woman called out. She was dressed as a pink witch, with a wig that looked as if it was made from candy floss, topped with a small pink pointed hat on a headband. "I've been waiting for you," she said, then frowned at me and put her hands on her hips. “Who are you?”

“Becky,” I said with a sigh. Walking around the ball with Connor was a bad idea, I felt I was being attacked and at this rate I’d never find my friends.

“We’re doing a charity project together,” Connor said. “Called Cat Lovers.”

“You’re late,” she said ignoring what he had said.

Connor let go of my arm, approached the petite woman and whispered something into her ear. She leaned up and kissed him full on the mouth. I decided this was my chance to slip away. It seemed to me that Connor Davies had a couple of complex relationships and I didn’t want to get caught in any cross-fire.

CHAPTER 4

I made my way to the Halloween Ball bar.

"Boss!"

I turned around to see Jeff coming out of a door marked 'no entry'.

"What are you doing?" I asked, looking at him and then at Iona who was also dressed in a matching ghost-catcher boiler-suit. To be honest, Iona needn't have bothered with an outfit, since she looked like she was dressed for Halloween on a normal day, with her black hair and dark gothic fashion.

"We slipped up to the turret. I've experienced a load of activity up there recently," Jeff said.

"Hi," Iona smiled at me and stuck her arm in Jeff's. She was much shorter than him and four years older, but there was a youthful appearance about her. Eager, that's how she came across.

I grinned at them. They looked great as ghost-hunters. Both had equipment packs on their backs, which Jeff had made himself from various items bought from the D.I.Y. store, where he worked part-time. Coming out of the packs were wide hoses to presumably suck ghosts with. Of course, this wasn't his real ghost hunting apparatus.

"Your outfits are amazing. Well done, Jeff."

I looked up at the stone stairs to the turret as static buzzed up my back.

"You can feel it, can't you?" Jeff said. "The paranormal activity."

"You really do have the gift," Iona said. "Jeff is always talking about it." I saw the whites of her eyes surrounded by very thick kohl eye-liner. "You're really sensitive to the spirits."

"It's probably Jeff's fault," I said. "He's woken them up with his monthly ghost-hunts."

He shook his head. "I think it's your gift developing. You're special, Becky. Come on, let's check it out together." He pulled his mobile phone from his pocket. He had a ghost hunting app on it which showed any spiritual being as a fluorescent stick man on the screen.

I looked behind me. As much as I hated ghost-hunting, I didn't like the atmosphere at the party one little bit. "Okay."

Iona gave a determined look and clutched her ghost sucking pipe, as if it really worked.

As we climbed the stairs of the turret, the buzzing

sensation I felt, became quite painful and I regretted my decision. I felt a breeze across my face as we reached the room within the turret.

"We're always up here, it's the most active place," Jeff said. "I've read up on the history of the castle." He passed his E.M.F meter to Iona. "There have been sightings of six different spirits at the castle over recent years. I've picked them up on the equipment but have not visited with anyone who's gifted enough to see them."

"Jeff's always saying how he wants you here for a proper hunt," Iona said. "Although, I'm working on developing my gift too."

"Are you feeling anything?" Jeff asked me.

I nodded. "It's intense." I yelped as a nip of static grabbed my neck. "What about Lynn? She could come up with you and take messages."

"I asked, she wasn't interested. She only wants to help people connect with their relatives."

I nodded. "Us natural mediums always have our set uses. I'm usually contacted by spirits if there's an injustice. And as you know, I really don't like it. Ouch." I jumped as I felt a sharp sensation like a large needle scraping down my back. I saw movement out of the corner of my eye. "They're here," I whispered.

"Something's floating across my screen." Jeff stared eagerly at his smartphone, then showed it to Iona.

The E.M.F. meter, which Iona held in her hand

emitted bleeps and signals confirming a change in the electromagnetic field.

Iona stared up at Jeff as if he was a superhero, then at me with her eyes wide open.

I stopped still, as a lady in a long black dress whooshed up to me.

Taking a quick step backwards, I pressed myself against the cold stone wall of the turret and my witches hat fell off. I was hit by a burst of fear and not all mine. It was coming from the spirit.

"Beware," the spirit whispered. I could feel her icy breath in my ear. "The woman in black kills. Run. Save yourself."

She disappeared through the wall.

Jeff stood, mouth agape, staring at me.

I was speechless, as static fizzed all over my body.

Iona's eyes were wide open. "What happened?"

I shuddered. "I don't like this. I need to get out of here." I bent down and retrieved my hat.

"What did you see?" Jeff asked eagerly.

I decided against giving him the details, I knew he would have dragged me around the whole castle to find out what each and every one of the resident spirits had to say. And Iona's excitement was a little disconcerting. "Nothing," I said. "I just sensed something." I shuddered, disturbed by what the spirit had told me.

"You look shocked, Becky. Are you sure they didn't say something?" Iona asked, seemingly seeing straight through me.

I didn't want to lie but neither did I want to be dragged into something. "As I've explained to Jeff before, connecting to a spirit isn't just about seeing them, it's about absorbing their emotions and it can be disturbing, It gives you feelings, which can stay with you for a while. It can be quite shocking, no matter how brief."

"I can tell your gift has moved to a new level," Jeff said. "I wish you would grab your destiny and make it into something. We could do so much together." His ultimate goal was to have his own You Tube ghost-hunting channel.

"I don't want to be world famous," I said. I cringed every time Izzy wrote an article about me in the local press.

"I'm always telling Iona, you have so much potential, aren't I, baby?" he said throwing a look at his girlfriend, no doubt for back-up with his sales pitch.

Iona nodded. "Jeff thinks he could make millions if you got more involved in the business."

I sighed. "And as I've told Jeff, so many times, a life in the public eye is not for me. I was not bestowed this gift to be some sort of freak-show entertainer." I heard the tone of my voice had changed. The underlying current of grump was rising to the surface, so I stuck a smile on my face. I needed to calm down, it wasn't Jeff and Iona's fault that I was fed up with H. "Let's get back to the party."

As we travelled downstairs, I heard Jeff whispering

to Iona that he thought I was going to cave in. I wasn't, but ignored him, deciding to make my point even clearer when we got home, and Iona wasn't in earshot.

Once out of the turret, I calmed down. I thought of the spirit I had seen, realising she was probably a ghost, replaying the same words, night in and night out. A footprint left on the world, which never fades through time. *Maybe she was killed by a woman in black, centuries ago?* I thought. On the other hand, heeding her warning to run away, was justification for me to leave the party early. There were a lot of women there dressed in black. I was not in the mood for dancing and just wanted to go home and curl up with Constance in the snug and catch a late film. And not a spooky one.

I turned to Jeff and Iona, "I'll find Annie, Lynn and Dannie, say hi and then make my way home. I'm feeling tired and not really in the party mood. Have a great evening, guys."

I waved to them as they went towards another door, no doubt deciding to do more ghost hunting. I scanned the room for Annie and Wes. As I did, I saw Connor dancing with a woman dressed in a black sequinned dress with a devil-horned headband and a whip. She seemed to be monopolising him as she pulled him close, then pushed him away in a very seductive fashion. Looking around, I noticed the pink witch, with her arms crossed, frowning at Connor and his dance partner. It was true what Annie said, he did seem to have a lot of girlfriends and I didn't really have to worry about Connor having designs on me. He was clearly a man who liked to flirt – shamelessly. *And by the looks of it, he's getting away with it,* I thought. The devil he was dancing with suddenly slapped his face and stormed off the floor.

Hmm, I thought. *Maybe not.*

Connor laughed, then walked away in the opposite direction, without even rubbing his face, which must have stung. As I watched him, I noticed a man staring at me. He was on his own and dressed as Frankenstein, but I was sure that I recognised him behind the make-up. Mind you, a lot of people came through my café. I rubbed static away from my neck as I scanned the room again for Annie and when I turned back, Frankenstein was walking away, his gait also appeared familiar.

The D.J. changed track and I spotted Annie and Wes on the dance floor, strutting their stuff to the famous zombie choreography in their ripped outfits. I smiled, they were the best-looking zombies in the house. And if there was a competition for the best dressed, they would have got my vote. They totally nailed the dance. I laughed as I watched them, they really cheered me up. When they were finished, I met them at the top of the steps.

"You guys owned that dance floor," I said.

"Where's H?" Annie asked panting from her dance.

I shook my head. "No surprises, he blew me out." I

was fed up with explaining that he was tied up with the case, then felt guilty at the way I'd said it. I knew how hard he worked and our long-term relationship may well be doomed, but he was dedicated to his job. And the Mayor of Exeter had been murdered and it was right that H found the killer. A death was slightly more important than a fancy dress ball. *Did I overreact?* I asked myself? Telling him it was over? *Probably.* I wished I'd not reacted in such a knee-jerk fashion when I had texted him back. I realised that my urge to go home, was so that I could get my phone and apologise.

I felt an arm snake around my shoulder.

Annie grinned.

I turned to see it was Connor.

"Mr Davies, great threads," Wes said, looking him up and down.

"Thank you, Wes. Would you two like a drink? I'm just taking this beautiful witch to the bar."

"I was on my way home, actually," I said.

"I won't allow it." He grabbed hold of my hand.

I felt it was going to be a long evening.

CHAPTER 5

Conner had bought drinks from the cocktail bar which was situated at the end of the dance floor. Annie and Wes got talking to friends, leaving me with Connor. I took a large gulp of my Pina Colada. I have to say it was absolutely delicious with sweet coconut cream, mixed with fruity pineapple and a hint of rum. I savoured the drink, it felt comforting and calmed me from my ghostly experience. The static was still there and a hint of the emotions which I had connected to. But there was no sharp stabbing pain in my body.

I looked out to the dance floor and smiled. I knew a good few people there and felt as if I was a real part of the community. Elena Corelli who owned my favourite restaurant was dancing with Andrew Farr and Katherine Sherringham who ran the funfair and pier. And the Mayor and Mayoress otherwise known as

Nigel and Gina Levison were there, although were part of a small percentage of people who had not joined in with the fancy dress.

I turned my head as I felt a nip of static in my neck. A man approached, dressed as a gangster. He had a pock-marked face, and while it was not a traditional Halloween outfit, there was something menacing about it.

"Davies," he said.

Connor turned around. "What are you doing here?"

"Same as everyone else."

"Stop following me." Connor pointed at him. "If I see you in my face again, you'll regret it." I was shocked at the instant change in Connor. From charming to outright terrifying. The ice blue eyes had frosted over and his mouth had curled.

I gulped.

"I'm just making sure you're keeping to your side of the deal," the man said.

"Don't try to intimate me, Spud. You can't." Connor gave him a sneer which set the static off in my neck. I felt like a spare part and began to inch away until Connor gabbed by hand to prevent my escape, without taking his eyes off Spud.

I steadied myself as I nearly spilt my drink.

Spud's eye twitched. "Mr Angel sends his regards for your health." He nodded at me and moved away.

"Who's that?" I asked as I retrieved my hand, feeling my palms become sweaty.

"He's from a firm in Bath. Goes by the nickname of Spud after he punctured a rival's head with various objects." Connor took a mouthful of his Old Fashioned.

"What?" I put a clammy hand to my throat. "Like Mr Potato head?"

Connor nodded. "Exactly that."

"And by firm, do you mean a crime ring?"

"If you want to call it that."

"But Bath is so nice," I said as I took another sip of my drink.

"There are bad people in every town."

"Not in Branden Bay," I said.

Connor remained silent and stared at me over his drink. A realisation seeped into me that maybe I was looking at the new crime lord of Branden Bay. Maybe the charity shop was his way of widening the net from Bristol to Branden. *Oh no,* I thought. I wasn't the face of a charity shop, I was the cover-girl for a crime ring. And Constance was the cover cat! I gulped a mouthful of my coconut flavoured drink. Would Connor be going around the streets asking for contributions from all the shop owners? Would he bother my friend Elena for danger money? Would he attempt to buy off the Mayor and Mayoress?

Connor threw his head back and laughed as if he'd read my mind. "That's what I love about you, Becky, your wild and vivid imagination, which is written all over your face. My sister would never speak to me again if I did any business here, other than the charity shop. And I love her too much. Family is important."

I wasn't convinced. I looked away, feeling someone staring at me. It was the woman with the devil horns. She ran her whip through her hand and I remembered the voice of the ghost in my head.

The woman in black kills. Run. Save yourself.

I scanned the room, there were a few women wearing black at the ball, and even though the ghost was repeating words she may well have uttered for centuries, I'd had enough. I'd been at the ball for well over an hour. I'd shown my face. It was time to go home. I gulped down the remnants of my drink.

"Getting into the party mood, are we?" Connor said. "I'll get you another."

"No, Connor. I'm not really feeling it. I've had enough."

"You need to forget about the policeman. I can make you happy." He took my hand.

I laughed. "Connor, I've seen how you are with women. I don't think I could hack it."

"No other woman is as enigmatic as you." He lifted my hand to his lips then kissed it.

"Admit it, Connor. You just like the chase and, as flattered as I am, you'd drop me as soon as you took a bite," I said staring at his fangs. "But never mind that, because I really want to go home."

"One dance, then I'll ask my driver to drop you back."

"Ok," I said. It sounded like a compromise to me, and I'd have a lift. I didn't fancy walking home late on Halloween night, by myself.

As we passed the D.J, Connor gestured at him. While I didn't catch what he said, I knew I'd been had when we reached the dance floor and a slow song came on — *The Lady in Red*."

"Ah, great timing," Connor said.

"Isn't it just?" I had to laugh, though, Connor was trying hard.

He took my arms and held me in a traditional ballroom hold. Which I was pleased about. I didn't want to get too up close and personal.

"You should wear red," he said.

"It'd clash with my hair." I looked over his shoulder. I saw Dannie, sipping a drink and watching me and I nodded at her, pleased that I had at least caught her eye. She frowned as she watched me dancing with Connor and I guessed she was concerned.

As Connor twirled me around, I noticed that Dannie wasn't the only person frowning. The devil in the black sequin dress, was also staring at us.

"Who's that woman you were dancing with, in the sequinned dress with the horns?" I asked as he pulled me close.

He pushed me back and swung me around, groin to groin. My hat had no hope of staying on and fell to the floor. He brought me up close again. "It's Sofia, she's a fashion designer."

"I don't think she likes me dancing with you."

"It's me she has a problem with. We're through. I think she's got the message."

A guy dressed as a skeleton handed me my hat and I held it between my hand and Connor's as we danced.

I noticed the pink witch, scowling at us with her arms crossed. "I don't feel very popular, at all," I said to Connor.

Izzy danced by with Martha who gave Connor the daggers, and his feline ex-wife stood at the side, with one hand on her hip, shaking her head at us. As the song came to a close, I disentangled myself from Connor and made my way off the dance floor. I pitied anyone who was interested in a relationship with him, it would be a one-way trip to a broken heart.

As soon as we were off the dance floor, Connor took my hand and pulled me close. "I wish you would let me take you somewhere European."

I felt my stomach rumble, realising I'd totally forgotten to eat. "I have to admit," I said. "I wish Corelli's was open, I love their lasagne."

Connor laughed. "I meant a country not a restaurant. Would you like me to take you away? A week in paradise. A remote island?" He whispered in my ear. "I'd love to snorkel with you." He leaned back and stared into my eyes, winking at me. He certainly made snorkelling sound as if it was something a lot more intimate than watching tropical fish.

I gulped. "Er ... thanks for the offer," I squeaked.

"You will?" He stroked my hair. "I have dreamed of this for months. And then after the beach we can come back via a city. Maybe Venice, and I can shower you with gifts."

Connor was really getting carried away. I'd only said I wished I was in Corelli's stuffing my face with Italian food.

"And when we get back, we can find somewhere to live. Do you think our cats will get along?"

This was ridiculous. I stared at him and he threw his head back in a vampire laugh.

"Oh, you're joking," I said with relief.

He pulled me close again. "I was, but if you'd said yes, I'd have jetted you away in a heartbeat. I've never met anyone like you before. Stop waiting around for someone that will always put his job first. I've made my money, I'm ready to get serious and to spoil the perfect woman."

I opened my mouth to defend H. Being a policeman was who he was and a part of him, it was a calling, his vocation. But I didn't want to discuss H, while I still felt upset and I'd probably blown it with him.

"And now, I'll let you go," Connor said.

As he released me, Lynn approached. "Are you

okay, lovey?" She was dressed as a bright orange pumpkin, which she'd knitted herself.

"Yes." I nodded as I leaned back, in case her rotund outfit pushed me over.

"H didn't show then?" she said in a quiet voice.

"No, I'm off home now." I put my hat back on. "Connor is just calling his driver to meet me out the front." I gestured to Connor who had his phone to his ear.

"I don't blame you. The atmosphere in here is pretty tight."

Static nipped at my neck and I rubbed it with my hand.

"You feel it too?" Lynn said. "I wish I could leave with you, but my friend is enjoying herself, so I'll have to stay for at least another hour or two."

Connor arrived by my side and stuck his arm out. "I'll see you to the car."

Lynn bent forward, squidging her pumpkin against me and planted a kiss on my cheek. "Take care, lovey. I'll pop over tomorrow."

I took Connor's arm, pleased to be getting out of the place. I had the uncanny feeling of a thousand eyes upon me as we walked towards the door.

Once outside, I shivered wishing I'd worn a coat. I hadn't thought of that when I'd stomped up there in a rage. I looked down at the foot of the steps where Connor's white Hummer was positioned, illuminated by the full moon, which was covered in wispy clouds, as if it was also dressed for Halloween.

"Thank you," I said, relieved that Connor did not insist on coming home with me. I guessed he was planning on spending the evening with one of his admirers.

"Do I get a kiss goodbye?" he asked.

Let's shake hands," I replied. "After all, we're associates working on a charity venture."

I stretched out my hand and he took it, pulling me close, looking deep into my eyes, half an inch from my face so I could smell the whisky cocktail he had drunk. He remained there for what felt like forever, with me in a vice-like hold. I could not move and I realised that if he did try to kiss me, there was no way I'd be able to dodge it.

I heard something whizz by, like a firework.

A dull ache filled the top of my arm.

A loud crack sounded as I felt myself falling, still in Connor's arms.

I heard someone call my name. "Becky!"

Is that H? I thought, before losing consciousness.

CHAPTER 6

I prised my eyelids open. Bright light flooded my vision. I shut them again, as a shooting pain hit the back of my sockets.

Oh my head, I thought as a dull nausea washed around my stomach. I felt dizzy. *I must have drunk way too much.* I wracked my brain, trying to remember where I had been and what I had done. My mind was hazy.

I heard a voice and opened my eyes again. But I was not in my bedroom. "Where am I?" I croaked, totally confused.

"Becky. Thank God. Do you remember what happened?"

Is that H? I thought as I moved my head to the side.

"You're probably concussed," he said.

I tried to lift my right arm, but, *ouch.* It hurt. I relaxed and breathed deeply, attempting to clear the fog from my mind. The memories filtered in. I was at the Halloween Ball. I was saying goodbye to Connor, he had me in a vice like hold inches from his face and I was bracing myself as I guessed he was going to kiss me. A couple of fireworks went off, then I'd heard H calling my name.

"Did I fall down the steps?" I asked.

"You were shot."

I bolted my eyes open and checked my arm. There was a large dressing on the top half. H was sitting on a chair, and I was in a hospital room. "Who by?"

"No-one knows and we've not yet located the gun. But you could have been killed. They were inside the room in the right hand turret and took aim through the slit window."

"But why?" I asked. "If it had happened when I was investigating a murder, I might have understood, but I've been keeping myself to myself." I scratched my head. "Do you think it's to do with the recent court cases we attended?" H and I had both been called to appear in two hearings.

He shook his head. "The culprits are both behind bars. It was likely to be something to do with your date, Connor Davies," he said through gritted teeth. "I told you before, to keep away from that man. Then I turn up to find you kissing him."

"I was not kissing him, he was just ... close."

"Were you going home with the guy?" A frown topped his dark eyebrows above even darker eyes.

"No. He was just getting me a lift. There's nothing going on. He's just a touchy-feely guy."

"That's not how he was described by the force."

"Was?" I sat up and winced at the pain coming from my arm.

H looked at the door then back at me. "He got a bullet in his back. Thank God, otherwise it would have ended up inside you. They're operating on him now, but his expected outcomes are not great."

My eyes smarted with tears. "He's going to die?"

"Becky. I told you before, he lives in a different world to us. One in which fatalities happen as a matter of course. It was probably a hit by a rival gang."

"But he was so nice to me." I sat back in the bed, feeling pain in my arm as I moved. I couldn't quite believe it. Connor, so full of life and charming, although with an edge, was fighting for his life and by the look on H's face, it was possible he was already dead. "He was just about to open a charity shop."

H shook his head. "Becky, he's a dangerous and warped man. Why can't you accept that?"

"And what about Tara?" I asked. "He's her brother, she must be beside herself with worry."

A doctor entered the room. "Great, you're conscious. How are you feeling Becky?" she asked.

"I have a headache and my arm is sore. I feel sick but that's probably because I'm worried about Connor. How is he?"

"Mr Davies is still in surgery."

I turned to H. "The police need to find out who did this." I looked out of the window and saw it was still dark. "How long have I been in here?"

"A few hours."

The doctor took my blood pressure and shone a light into my eyes. She made me drink a full glass of sweet orange squash and told H to leave soon and let me rest. Then she left the room.

"I want to know who did this," I said to H.

"The force checked everyone at the gate before they left. But no gun was found. They'll be searching high and low for it at the castle. Brad is travelling up from Cornwall as we speak."

Brad A.K.A. award-winning D.C.I. Bradley Harris, was not my greatest fan and I knew he would be seething at me, being involved in yet another case.

"He's not happy," H said.

"That's no surprise. He hates me."

"He's extra mad this time, being dragged away from a long weekend away with Smith."

Brad had been in a long-term relationship with one of his co-workers.

"He proposed," H said.

"They're getting married?" I asked. Brad didn't look like the settling down type.

H nodded. "Yep. Smith is pregnant and due to give birth in the new year."

"Wow. You kept that one a secret."

"I didn't know until today, as you know — I've been

in Devon. Seems they kept it quiet until it was impossible to disguise her bump."

I'd not seen Brad's girlfriend, Lucy Smith, since June when she would only have been a couple of months pregnant. "I can't imagine him as a dad."

"They're planning on moving to Branden Bay. Smith doesn't want either of them working on vice, now they're starting a family. She wants them both to be transferred here permanently, although he's only involved in this case because Connor Davies lives in Bristol and is on Brad's patch. He's always on his radar."

I groaned at the thought of the D.C.I. being a permanent fixture in Branden Bay. He was not fond of me and had arrested me on more than one occasion. He had threatened to charge me with wasting police time a couple of times, but let me off. I needed to steer clear of him because I knew there would be no further warnings.

"I have to leave now," H said.

"I thought you couldn't come back for the Halloween Ball?" I felt my face heat up, as I recalled the text I'd sent him, saying we should end it.

He took my hand. "I wasn't making a lame excuse, I have an extra body relating to my case, stored in Exeter morgue. But I drove up to say in person, that I'm serious about us having a relationship." He squeezed my hand. "I know I've neglected you, but I'm in the thick of a high-profile case. I'm serious about you and about us making a go of it. And I wanted to show you." He bent down and gave me an earth-moving kiss that left me feeling like I should grab for the oxygen.

I gave a small smile when he pulled away. "Me too. Sorry, I sent that text off before I'd thought it through. I tried to recall it, but you'd already read it."

"It's forgotten." He stood up. "I start work at eight." He shook his head. "If I'd come back and gone to the ball with you, you wouldn't have been with Davies, and wouldn't have been hurt in the crossfire. It's my fault."

"You can't take the blame," I said. "It's the shooter that's responsible."

He bent down and put his arms around me. "I thought I'd lost you."

I lifted my good arm and gave him half a hug.

"Now the doctor's orders are that you have to rest. You won't be alone once they discharge you." He gave me a squeeze then pulled away. "The hospital waiting room is fit to bursting with your friends. And Jeff is in the van with your cat." He stood up. "I'll let them know you're fine. But take care, Becky. I ..." He lifted my hand and paused, "... care." His eyes searched mine for a reaction.

I flushed hot. For a moment, I thought he was going to use the 'L' word. "I care too," I said. "Good luck with your case. You're a brilliant detective."

"I'll be back as soon as I can." He gave me a final peck on the forehead.

I laid my head back on the pillow, smiling until my

mind pulled up a picture of Connor. *I hope he pulls through,* I thought.

It wasn't until mid-morning that I was able to leave the hospital. I felt like a rock star as I walked out with an entourage. A rather odd entourage as we were still dressed in Halloween clothes. Izzy held my right hand and Annie held the other. Dannie carried meds, Blue held my witches hat, Wes walked ahead like a security escort and Lynn waddled behind us in her pumpkin, reading an information sheet provided by the hospital, dishing out orders to me about resting and not using any heavy machinery. I was aching, all over and had a few bruises from the fall.

I spotted Jeff's van and noticed Constance on the front dash, pawing at the window. My spirits lifted when I saw her. All I wanted to do was give her a hug.

I insisted going back in the van with Jeff and Wes helped me into the passenger seat.

Jeff smiled at me as Wes shut the van door. "I'm so pleased to see you, boss." His voice caught in his throat as he rubbed his scrappy beard. I could see his eyes were red from tears.

"Jeff, I'm fine."

Constance jumped onto my lap giving a low meow and rubbed her fluffy head against my face. I waved thanks to my friends with my good arm as they wearily clambered into a limo, which I assumed Izzy had hired.

"So, what happened?" Jeff asked as he put the van into gear.

"Connor saw me out of the castle." My memory had fully returned. "He was saying goodbye and I heard a whizz and a crack, it turned out to be a bullet fired from the room in the right hand turret, the one we were in earlier that evening. The first bullet slightly grazed my arm and the second entered Connor's back."

"They were searching everyone at the gates of the castle. It was insane up there, after word got around you'd been shot. H ordered security to shut the gates to the road."

"H says they haven't found the weapon."

"Iona sends her love."

"Thanks," I said as I stroked my cat, feeling calmer as I did so. "And don't worry, I'm fine, it's just a scratch."

"She's really shaken up. I felt bad leaving her." He swallowed. "I feel like I've let you down. I'm supposed to be the one who protects you."

"Hey, you can't be with me all the time!"

"It was mad there. People were rushing around screaming. The shooter must have been lost in the crowd. I wonder who it was?" Jeff said.

"Someone who hates Connor Davies." I winced as Jeff drove around the corner. "H seems to think it would have been a rival gang."

"That seems logical."

"Yes," I said, keeping the words that I had heard the spirit say, to myself. But they rang again in my ears – *the woman in black kills. Run. Save yourself.* I wanted to process what had happened before I allowed myself to be sucked into anything paranormal. After all, it may have had nothing to do with what happened to me. I turned to Jeff. "Does anyone know how Tara is?" I asked.

"She was crying when she saw Connor on the floor and went away with him in the ambulance. I guess she's in the surgery waiting room."

"I'll text Marcus when we get back. This is so awful. I hope they manage to save Connor." The thought appeared in my mind, that if he did die, he'd haunt me until I found the killer. I certainly wanted him to stay alive.

CHAPTER 7

After spending Sunday in bed, I got up on Monday morning and spent the day convalescing with Constance in the snug, which was what I called the small lounge at the back of my house. It had large French windows providing views of my garden. It was pelting with rain and I watched large droplets racing down the glass. I felt much better, even with the lump that had appeared on the back of my head, the bruises on my skin in various parts of my body and my bullet grazed arm. The concussion appeared to have been mild. Although my food mixer was far from heavy machinery, I decided to keep the café closed for a few days so didn't need to bake anything for the next day.

H had kept in touch and was sending me regular texts. I told him I was fine and had sent a couple of pictures of myself smiling in case he didn't believe me.

I flicked through the television channels when Dannie appeared at the door.

"Carol's here to see you."

Carol sidled past her. "Look at you my poor daughter." Carol, H's mother had been referring to me as her daughter-in-law before H and I had even got together. To say she had taken a shine to me was an understatement. She had a shock of dark hair with a blonde streak in her fringe and the same brown eyes as her son.

Dannie smiled. "I'll stick the kettle on and Jeff has made a batch of chocolate chip cookies." She returned to the kitchen, which was in the next room.

"I'm taking you back to my place," Carol said.

I laughed. "I'm fine here, honestly."

"What? With a mad gunman on the loose?"

Constance gave a loud meow.

"See," Carol said pointing at my cat. "Constance agrees and she can come too."

"She would love it, I'm sure, seeing as you're always feeding her double portions of salmon when we visit." I laughed. "But don't worry, Dannie and Jeff are looking after me."

"No-one looks after you as well as a mother. When are your parents getting back?"

"Next month," I said, realising it was now November.

"They must be beside themselves with worry, after what you've been through."

"I haven't told them."

"Why in heaven's name not?"

"There's nothing they can do. And I don't want them to worry."

"If it was my Henry that was injured, I'd be straight on the plane home."

"Exactly, they're on the last leg of their around the world trip and I don't want to ruin it."

"Where are they now?"

"Back in Europe. Last time they checked in, they were just about to board a yacht in Greece for a cruise around the islands."

"I still think they should know."

"Carol, don't spoil it for them."

She sat next to me and Constance jumped onto her lap. "I hope you're going to leave this to the police. That Connor Davies is bad news. Anyway, I've a slow cooker full of beef stew at home. I'll pop it round. You can share it with your housemates."

"I don't want to steal your evening meal?"

"Paul can have chips and egg for a change." She stroked Constance who settled down as Dannie and Jeff brought in the tea and cookies, which we enjoyed together.

Two hours later I watched an episode of a legal drama as the delicious waft of beef stew filled my home. I'd promised to visit Carol when H was next home. He was due back the following weekend, assuming no further dead bodies appeared on his patch.

I glanced up to see Lynn walking up my garden path, carrying an umbrella and wearing purple Wellington boots. I waved at her. There was a gate in the stone wall between our properties, which led to the spiritualist church she ran in an old scout hut. It was extra handy as Jeff was able to park the van there in the busy months when Beach Road, which ran parallel to the promenade, was full. That wasn't the case in the winter though, there was always a space outside my house.

The door to the snug opened and Lynn walked in, having come in via the kitchen. She had changed into slippers. "I have a late lunch here for you and some left-over Halloween carrot cake. I see you've a meal for tonight?"

"Yes, Carol dropped it by."

She joined me and Constance on the sofa.

"I texted Tara," I said, as I picked up a sliced beef sandwich. "Her brother is still fighting for his life. They've done all they can with the surgery and the rest is up to him."

"Lovey, if the rumours are true, then Mr Davies has lived life on the wrong side of the law. He must know some unsavoury characters. He chose his path. Now, you need to relax. You look stressed."

"I know, I tell you what I really want?" I said. "A long bath."

After we ate our sandwiches and cake, Lynn helped me to standing just in case I still felt dizzy, but my head was clear. She followed me up the stairs to make sure I did not fall and then left, saying she would be back as soon as I wanted to reopen the café.

After a long soak in the tub with lavender bubble bath, I felt a lot better and pulled a jumper on to cover up my bandaged arm, which I had managed to keep dry. I entered the kitchen. Inside I found Dannie, Jeff and Iona chatting at the table

"You look really well," Dannie said as she took a picture of me with her phone. "Blue was worried about you, so I'm just texting her this pic."

"You had us worried," Iona said. "Jeff was in a right mess."

I smiled at Iona, but I did feel a bit disappointed she was there in my kitchen. I felt a bit crowded but covered it up. Constance often reacted to my moods, and I didn't want her growling at Iona and giving the game away, that I wished she wasn't there. After all, Iona had done nothing wrong, it was up to me, to get used to Jeff having a girlfriend.

"What are you going to do about the case?" Jeff asked picking up my cat and ruffling her fur.

"The police think it was a gang thing. And that's way out of my league," I said. "And there's no ghost haunting me."

"But someone shot you," Jeff said.

"They shot Connor, she just got in the way," Dannie said.

The doorbell rang and Dannie rose to answer it, then returned with Marcus who approached me with his arms outstretched.

"No hugs, I've got a sore arm," I said before he reached me. "Now sit down and tell us everything you've heard." I made a fresh pot of tea. I felt better doing something, even if it was one-handed.

Marcus sat down and Constance jumped onto his lap. He leaned back gingerly and stroked the top of her head.

I laughed. "She's not going to bite you."

He slowly reached for a muffin from the ugly cake tin, where all the rejects were kept, although with the cafe closed it consisted of general left overs. He peeled off the paper case as he spoke. "It's not certain whether he'll survive. They said they expect him to be in intensive care for some time. But he has his own private room."

"Poor Connor," I said.

"How's Tara?" Dannie asked Marcus.

"She's camped up at the hospital and I've been overseeing the gym for her. She feels responsible as she gave Connor the ticket to the ball."

"And I was feeling guilty for allowing him to arrange a lift home for me," I said. "But it could have happened anywhere."

"Especially if there's a contract out on him," Jeff said.

"Has Tara said anything to the police?" I asked.

"That rough cop from Bristol spoke to her," Marcus said. "He said something on the lines of – people who live on the wrong side of the law, can't be surprised if they get hurt."

"D.C.I. Brad Harris isn't known for his bedside manner," I said.

"There's always the chance," Marcus added. "That if it was someone from a rival gang that shot him, Connor wouldn't want the police involved and would prefer to deal with it himself, when he's back on his feet."

A short silence followed. I guessed it was true, Connor did live in a world with different rules to those regular people lived by.

Marcus broke the silence. "Tara's planning to visit the casino tomorrow, to speak to the staff. Connor is a very hands-on manager."

"Wes told Annie that it's like a wake over there," I said.

We were interrupted by the café landline ringing.

Dannie answered the phone in the hall and then returned. "Sorry, Becky, but the police are coming over to take your statement at five."

"It's a bit late in the day, isn't it?" I said. I was planning on dishing dinner up at that time, with crusty bread.

I saw Marcus out with Constance at my heel and Jeff left with Iona at the same time.

I decided to meet the police in the café. I wanted the interview to be a two-way thing. I grabbed my phone and tapped in some questions of my own. I would be taking notes.

Sitting in the café, I scanned the room, which was still decorated in a Halloween theme and as I looked up, I noticed that real cobwebs were joining the fake ones. My body ached, there was no way I could get up there to brush them away. The decorations and dust would just have to stay. Constance had followed me in and made herself comfortable in her bed.

I stood up to let D.C. Wright in and unlocked the door. "Come in, I'm glad the D.C.I. isn't here."

She smiled. "He might still call you in, I'm afraid. He's not on the same team as me, yet. Although if rumours are true, he's moving to Branden Bay, so you'll have to keep out of his way."

I showed her to a table where I had placed a tea pot. "Have you any suspects?"

Wright laughed. "This visit is about you giving information to me, not the other way around."

I pointed to the plate. "Cookie?"

She took one. "So, how are you?"

"I have a few bruises from the fall but my arm feels much better, it was only a graze. But poor Connor." I poured out the tea.

"I understand that you spent some time with Mr Davies inside the event?"

I added milk to our cups. "I only spent about half an hour with him."

"And who did he speak to when he was there?"

I was about to launch into my run-down of events, then hesitated, wondering how Connor would react if I spoke about him to the police in detail. Would he consider me a snitch? A grass? I knew there were certain codes to live by in the criminal world. But then I was no criminal. And the police must know who was there, by the list of people who had bought tickets.

After a period of silence, Wright spoke again. "Okay, I understand that no-one speaks about Connor Davies. That man slips through our fingers on a regular basis. So, I'll be more specific. He was spotted speaking to Norman Waite and you were by his side at the time. What was said?"

"I don't know anyone of that name." That was true but I was guessing Norman might be Spud's real name. "Can you describe what he looked like?"

"Huge, rough skin and dark hair. We're pretty sure this attack was gang related and he's a member of a group in Bath, which is part of an on-going investigation. It would help, not only with this investigation but the wider case, if you could give me this information. Were any names mentioned?"

There was no way I was about to mention a Mr

Angel of the Bath firm. “I’m not sure, but I think it was a woman that shot us,” I said deflecting the question.

Wright frowned. “What makes you say that?”

The woman in black kills. Run. Save yourself. The voice echoed in my mind. “I saw a spirit there who warned me about a woman wearing black.”

“Okay,” Write said in a slow voice. “Maybe I’ll come back when your head has cleared from the concussion.” She drained her tea then stood up. “I know you must feel involved in this case because you were hit by a bullet, but it was not meant for you. Steer clear because these guys will think nothing of killing you or anyone else who gets in the way of their operation.”

I nodded, but as Constance hissed from her bed, I felt a nudge to call everyone together.

CHAPTER 8

The following evening, Lynn and Dannie set out tables in the café. I had invited all my friends over for a meal. It wasn't going to be a formal meeting with a murder board. I needed to get my head around recent events and decide whether it was worth me pursuing it. And with the café being closed, the house felt too big and too quiet. It was great to have everyone together. Elena had called in to see how I was, and I'd ordered a selection of pizzas from her. Her new waiter had popped them down to us.

"Those pizza's smell amazing. Shall I call Jeff?" Lynn asked as she placed the boxes on the table.

I shook my head. "He's not upstairs, he's at Iona's. He'll be back soon."

Constance hissed and I stared at her.

"Do you disapprove of Iona?" Lynn asked me with a laugh.

"Why do you say that?" I raised by eyebrows.

Dannie laughed. "The tone of your voice and Constance's reaction."

"It just feels weird for him to have a girlfriend," I said.

"When you're used to him being at your beck and call," Lynn added with her eyebrows raised.

"I know what you mean," Dannie said. "He does seem different."

"Exactly," I said and relaxed, at least it wasn't just me.

I stood up as a car drew up and Dannie opened the café door for Izzy who had been dropped off.

Annie wandered in from the hall, having come in via the back door as her apartment was a few doors up from the spiritualist hut.

"We'll give Jeff a couple more minutes and then I think we'll start on the pizza," I said.

He soon rushed in with his face flushed and we all tucked into Picante and Margarita.

"So, sweetie, what are you going to do about the shooting? What are your thoughts?" Izzy asked.

I sat back in my seat. "The police are convinced that this is a job by a gangster and that's possible. Their prime suspect is Norman Waite, also known as Spud – he likes sticking items into his victims, as if they are Mr Potato head."

"That's horrific, sweetie, you really need to be careful," Izzy said.

Constance sashayed over to us from her cat bed with a loud meow.

"Did anyone else see a guy there, who looked like a bouncer?" I asked looking at my friends.

They stared back with blank expressions.

"To be honest, we were all enjoying the party," Dannie said. "What do you know about this man?"

"He works for a crime lord in Bath, who he referred to as Mr Angel."

Izzy nodded. "Damien Angel owns Ripples night club, in the centre of town. I'll look into the archives at work and see what I can find on him, if you like?" Izzy said.

"Thanks, I need to get a look at this guy."

"Are you mad?" Annie said. "I agree with the police you can't go over there."

"I can go with you," Jeff said eagerly.

Annie huffed.

"She's right, lovey," Lynn said to me. "It doesn't sound like the sort of place you should visit on your own."

"I want to get a look at this Angel guy, to see if I can sense anything. To be honest, I'm pretty sure it's not him. The ghost up at the castle told me to beware of a woman who dresses in black, not a man."

"Wait, what?" Jeff said through a mouthful of pizza. "The spirit in the turret spoke to you? And you didn't tell me?" He wiped his mouth on a napkin.

"No, I didn't. Because you and your *girlfriend,* would

be selling tickets for people to come and watch me at the castle communicating with the dead."

Constance gave an angry hiss from my side and jumped onto my lap.

Jeff's jaw dropped, and he lowered his head. I realised I'd near spat the words out.

Lynn shook her head at me.

I'd been too harsh.

"What spirit did you see, lovey?" Lynn asked in a gentle voice trying to smooth over the tension.

"A lady, in the right-hand turret, where the shot came from."

"Lady Astrid of Cleve is said to haunt that tower. She's an old ghost lovey, so is likely to be on repeat muttering words she has uttered for centuries."

I nodded. "That's what I thought at the time, that it could relate to something that happened hundreds of years ago to her and have nothing to do with me."

"What did she say, exactly?" Jeff asked in a quiet voice.

I softened my tone. "She warned me about a woman wearing black and told me she kills and to run."

"I've got the tingles," Lynn said. "Maybe we should go up there?"

"I've got the castle booked for this Friday night, I've let the hunters know it was cancelled, out of respect. But if the police have cleared out by then, we can go up there," Jeff said.

"We could all go," Annie said with wide eyes.

"Er, count me out," Dannie said wiping her hands on a napkin

"This is going to be a huge story," Izzy said as she took her notebook from her bag.

"No," I said. "I think it's best if we keep this visit low key. I don't want us all traipsing up there and creating attention." I also didn't want Jeff's girlfriend and his whole ghost hunting tribe following me around.

Izzy frowned. "So I can't have the story?"

"Of course, you can. I'll keep you all in the loop," I said. "If we decide to go forward with an investigation, then we can meet again next week. But first, I want to see if there's a case to follow, or if the police are right, and that it was a gang shooting and not something we can pursue. In which case Brad would be right and we'll have to leave it to the police."

"Sounds the sensible thing to do, lovey," Lynn added.

"I can go up to the castle with Jeff to see what else the spirit has to say."

"I'd better come, though," Lynn said. "To ensure the place has been swept of evil before you start."

I nodded. "Yes please, just the three of us." I looked at Jeff hoping that he had clocked that I didn't want Iona there.

He smiled and I smiled back.

Constance meowed loudly.

"Okay, the four of us," I said and the others laughed relaxing the atmosphere.

I yawned when Lynn ushered everyone out, then let herself and Annie out the back way. Dannie went up to her room leaving me alone with Jeff.

"Sorry I snapped at your earlier," I said. "This experience has rattled my nerves."

"No worries, boss, you've been shot. The thing about a woman in black is interesting, though. Do you have a suspect in mind? Were there any women in black that spoke to Connor when you were with him?"

I nodded. "But there must have been over a hundred women there dressed in black, with it being Halloween."

"Who spoke to him when you were there?"

"To start there was Tara, she was wearing black but as she's his sister she clearly wouldn't shoot him. Then we spoke to Izzy and Martha. Izzy was wearing white, and again, not a killer."

"What was Martha wearing?"

"Black and she did give Connor a hard stare. But she didn't speak to him and he didn't act as if he knew her."

"He's well known in Bristol and in Branden Bay, since he bought that empty shop.

"Yes, it's not just the Council that don't approve of him." I sighed. "I guess no-one wants a gangster opening a shop in the High Street."

"Who else did you meet at the ball?"

"We bumped into his wife, soon to be ex, called Helen Davies. She was wearing a black catsuit."

"Has Connor spoken about her?"

"He said he's just about to finalise their divorce and that it had taken a long time to go through. The sticking point is to do with finances."

"Do they have children?"

"Wes told Annie that the rumour around the casino is that Connor has had the snip, so that he can't get anyone pregnant. He likes women by the sounds of it and doesn't want to get caught out."

Jeff raised his eyebrows. "He's not even that good looking."

"He clearly has a magnetic appeal." I said.

"Was there anyone else?"

"A woman dressed as a pink witch."

"I guess she wasn't wearing black," Jeff said.

"No. But she did seem a bit desperate to be with him. There was definitely something odd about her, I'll try and find out who she is."

"Anyone else?"

"Yes, a woman dressed in a black sequin dress with devil horns. Connor said she was a fashion designer called Sofia. She became angry with him and slapped his face."

"Izzy might know her, with her modelling background."

"Good thinking, I'll ask her."

"So, we've got three days until we can access the castle. Do you want me to do anything before then?"

"You can take me over to the hospital tomorrow. I want to see if I can speak to Connor. He'll be able to fill in some details for me and he might have an idea if it was indeed a hit by a gang member." I smiled at Jeff, as Constance sat purring on his lap. It was great to have spent time with him, going over the details in my mind and I realised, I didn't really have a problem with Iona, I just missed spending time with Jeff. He felt like family and with Grandma gone and my parents away on their extended trip — for me, family was in short supply.

CHAPTER 9

I felt much brighter the following day when Jeff dropped me at the hospital. But when I met Tara in the waiting room, she told me that Connor was slipping in and out of consciousness and suggested we leave him for a while and go to the hospital café to talk .

"I'm so pleased you came," Tara said as we sat down at a table with our drinks. "No-one really cares about Connor. He's quite high on the medication they've given him. Assuming you're able to speak to him later, excuse anything odd he says. Whenever he wakes, he insists that I invite you in, but I didn't want to bother you, seeing as you were dragged into this mess and could have died in the crossfire." She looked me in the eye. "Connor has many associates but not many true friends. And I've not let any of his crazy women in. They've been buzzing around the hospital and messaging me on social media, asking if they can see him."

"I don't blame Connor for what happened to me," I said. "And it was only a minor wound."

"I think he wants to apologise, but in case he doesn't ..." She stopped. I knew she was going to say *in case he doesn't make it and dies*. Tara clearly loved her brother, for all her attempts to distance herself from his business dealings, he was her flesh and blood. "I've always told him to be careful and that I was scared something like this would happen." Her voice trembled and she spent a couple of seconds composing herself before she continued. "But still, it's not right for someone to shoot him. And I'm giving you an apology on his behalf. How's your arm?" she asked smoothing her chestnut hair which was tied in a ponytail.

"Much better," I said glancing at my arm. "The dressing is off and it just looks like a burn."

"What does H think about all of this?" she asked.

"He's out of town and obviously wants me to keep away from Connor. How are you holding up?"

"I'm fine, just worried about my big brother. They've got him in a separate I.C.U. room and there's a police guard on his door." She paused. "It doesn't look like they intend to investigate, and the guard is probably there to protect the staff, rather than my poor brother. He's not as bad as his reputation, Becky. A lot of it is bravado, to keep his rivals at bay. He's no saint, but it's disgusting the way the police are so dismissive."

"They sent a detective to the house to interview me. I don't think they're ignoring it, as such but they're focusing on their existing investigations into crime rings."

"Trust me, they're not bothering."

"Just to add, I told the police nothing when they asked me about the Bath firm and Spud," I added quickly. "Who do you think did it?"

"The Bath firm are contenders, but I don't see what the point would be of killing Connor, when their henchman made himself so visible at the ball."

"I agree. I haven't mentioned this to anyone else, but a few days before the Halloween Ball, I met Connor at the shop he owns in the High Street and there was someone watching us. A man and he took a picture."

Tara frowned. "What did he look like?"

"Dark hair, late thirties, wearing an antique leather jacket. It wasn't the henchman from Bath. Maybe he was working for someone else. I have a gut feeling that it was a woman that shot at us."

"Why do you say that?" Tara frowned.

"At the castle I saw a female spirit, in the turret. The same turret we were shot from. She said to beware of a woman in black who kills."

Tara stared at me. "I've always been a bit sceptical of your paranormal claims, but you've been spot-on before. I know Connor has always followed your cases with interest."

"The thing is, there were a lot of women at the ball dressed in black. Did Connor have any dealings with Martha Pine?"

"The artist?" she asked.

"Yes,"

"Not that I know of."

I felt a pang of guilt, as if I was spreading gossip about a friend. "I want to ask Connor about Martha, a fashion designer called Sofia who slapped him. Plus a woman dressed as a pink witch."

Tara sighed. "My brother has a few admirers. All of them, total nut jobs."

"And is wife, Helen?"

"Their divorce settlement is never ending," Tara said.

"What would happen if Connor died before it was settled?"

"The entire estate won't go to Helen, as he changed his will. It's coming to me and there would be a large donation to *Save the Cats*."

"But it would be easier for Helen to contest her share of the business, if he was dead," I said.

Tara nodded. "Probably, but I'm not sure she would kill him. Helen knew what Connor was like before she married him, she always blamed herself for what happened to her, acknowledging that she was foolish to think a wedding ring would change his ways. It didn't."

"It's often a motive for murder though – money. I'm guessing the grounds for divorce were adultery?"

Tara nodded. "As for the others, I didn't notice a pink witch at the ball. I'll see if I can find out from Connor who she was and let you know."

"And the clothes designer?"

"That's Sofia Arbello. She's had a casual fling with Connor for some time. When she's in town, she calls on him. She lives in Bath and travels the world with her shows, Connor used to host them but stopped a year ago when the divorce negotiations with Helen turned nasty. Sofia's been asking me to allow her to visit Connor. She said they had an argument and she won't rest until she apologises to him in person. She's staying up at Millar's but I'm not keen on her, so I've said no."

I tapped Sofia's full name into my phone's notes app. "Thanks, I've got enough to be going along with. I just need to see if I can speak to him."

After we finished our drinks, Tara led me to his private room.

The guard on the door nodded at us as we entered. I stopped in my tracks. Connor seemed so lifeless in the bed. Tara went up to him and smoothed his hair, which was usually sleeked back. He was on oxygen and was propped up at a slightly elevated angle in the bed.

Tara beckoned me over. "Becky's here," she said quietly to him.

He lifted his hand towards me, and I moved forward and took it.

Tara stepped to the side to give me space.

"Connor, do you know who did this to you?" I asked.

He shook his head. "Find ... the ... shooter." His eyes shut and he lost consciousness.

THE HOSPITAL VISIT was too much too soon for me and I'd spent the next two days at home resting. I reopened the café on Thursday. Izzy's article had also been published that day, which resulted in a surge of customers. The newspaper had a picture of myself and Connor on the front page with the heading, *Cat Lovers Shot at Haunted Castle.* The word 'cat' had a feline-face in place of the 'a' and it didn't look much like a word at all. At a glance, the heading read *Lovers Shot at Haunted Castle.* And the photograph Izzy had taken made it look as if we were a couple. I guessed Izzy's editor had done that on purpose, to sell more newspapers.

A few customers had asked if my 'boyfriend' was out of hospital yet. I hoped H hadn't seen it, as the newspaper covered the entire southwest, not just Branden Bay.

By Friday, my wound was healing well and the bruises had all come out. Whilst they looked awful, they didn't hurt so bad and my head was totally clear with no pain. Even better, the police forensics and search team had cleared out of Branden Bay Castle, although H told me that no gun had been located.

Our plan to go up and make contact with the spirit of Lady Astrid of Cleve was on. I thought it unlikely the police would uncover much from the scene, as the castle was usually open daily to the public and must have been full of D.N.A.

After nightfall, Jeff, Lynn, myself and Constance climbed into Jeff's van.

"Why do we have to go up there at night?" I asked as Jeff started the engine.

"People prefer ghost hunting in the dark," Jeff said. "That's why this slot is booked. It's exciting."

"That's not what I'd call it," I said as we began the journey up Castle Road.

"I've had loads of interest since Izzy's article was published," Jeff said. "Yesterday my phone was so busy, I'm booked up until Christmas. I might even be able to give up my job at the D.I.Y. store. I've spoken to the castle managers and I'm waiting to hear if I can book extra days, so I can run two hunts a week, instead of the one.

Once we arrived in the carpark, I climbed out of the van and looked up at the castle. It was a miserable night with the wind blowing in off the sea and my face was being basted with rain. It was way too windy for an umbrella. I stuffed Constance into my tote bag and walked towards the castle steps. She popped her head out and gave a loud meow as she looked up at the dark building. There were no lights at all projected onto it.

"Iona was giving me a hard time," Jeff said. "She wanted to come too, she'd booked the evening off work."

"This isn't a fun ghost hunt, it's serious," I said.

"I know, I explained that to her."

I wished I shared as much enthusiasm as Jeff's girlfriend for ghost hunts. I could see they were well suited, and I needed to back off with my disapproval.

I began to climb the steps and Constance wailed from my bag. I probably shouldn't have brought her but I felt calmer when she was with me. With the wind on my back, I felt as if I was being urged on by spiritual forces. As I looked behind me and down the steps, a picture flashed into my mind, of the whizz of the bullet and crack of the gun and of H calling my name. I took a deep breath. I hadn't factored in that I was revisiting a location where I was shot and would have an emotional reaction to that.

Lynn put her arm around me. "Come on lovey, let's get inside."

At the top of the steps, Jeff's keyring jangled as he found the right one. The door creaked as he opened it.

Once the four of us were inside, Jeff shut the door behind us. "We have to lock ourselves in, there's no security guard here."

He was interrupted by his E.M.F. meter, which began to pick up activity.

"Shall we go straight to the turret?" I asked. "I want to get this done. I've no desire to stop and chat with every spirit walking these halls."

Constance jumped to the floor and moved ahead of us, with her body close to the floor. As we reached doorways, she snaked around them. It put me on edge as my nerve endings fizzled. Without the distractions, of the people and music that were there on the night of the ball, I felt every fizz of every spirit present, and the place felt crowded with paranormal activity.

"I sense there's a lot here lovey," Lynn said. "Let's stop and pray to protect ourselves, before we connect to anything."

I wanted to go home but reminded myself, Connor was in a critical position and I wanted to help. We needed to explore whether a woman had committed the crime. Hopefully, we would collect more clues from Lady Astrid of Cleve.

We held hands with Constance in the centre and Lynn spoke some calming words asking for positive forces to protect us.

I opened my eyes. "Can you see anything Lynn?" I asked.

"I've seen a few shadows and orbs. They're watching us. I suggest we don't try to make contact until we're in the turret, otherwise we may have a long evening ahead of us. Remember the things I've taught you," Lynn said to me. "About distancing yourself, I can already feel much negative energy around here."

I nodded. Lynn had been helping me with my gift, to distance the emotions of those I made contact with. As we followed Jeff up the steps to the turret, I realised my senses were as alert as ever, as the static buzzed up my back in painful spasms and Constance wailed a low meow.

The buzzing intensified. "I can feel something. It's really close," I said as the static danced in my palms like sharp needles.

The E.M.F. meter bleeped frantically, and Jeff pulled out his phone and opened his ghost hunting app. "Tell me when you see something."

As we reached the room in the turret, I saw her immediately.

Constance hissed and her fur bushed out so much she reminded me of Lynn's Halloween pumpkin outfit.

The spirit rushed up to me.

"She's here," I said taking a step backwards. "The same lady I saw on the night of the ball."

"Beware," she whispered.

I gulped again, feeling her icy spirit breath in my ear.

"The woman in black kills. Run. Save yourself."

"Are you Lady Astrid of Cleve?" Lynn called out, looking in my direction.

I watched as the ghost seemed to be pulled towards Lynn who had her hands outstretched, as if trying to gravitate the spirit towards her.

Lynn paused. "I've got confirmation. It's definitely her."

"Who is the woman in black?" I asked in a whisper as I stepped away from the wall towards the spirit, hearing Constance wail at my feet. Part of me did not want Lady Astrid's spirit to speak, the other really needed to know who shot Connor and me.

The spirit pushed herself away from Lynn and circled me, I felt as if I was caught in an electric mini tornado. "Jealousy eats her," she screamed, then in a whoosh, she disappeared down the stairs.

I puffed out with a hand to my chest and leaned against the cool stone wall. "She's gone." I turned to Lynn and shuddered. "Did you hear what she said to me?" I asked.

She shook her head. "She wouldn't communicate with me. My spirit guide confirmed it was Lady Astrid. But I sensed her pain."

"I read that the man she loved was killed," Jeff said, wide-eyed. "And then she committed suicide, she hung herself in this turret." He looked upwards.

I followed his gaze to see a hook imbedded in the ceiling and gulped.

Lynn nodded. "That's what the tale says. And that was the level of pain I sensed from her." She shook herself as if to shake off the emotions, like a dog having exited the surf on the beach. "I felt an intense sense of loss. What did she say to you Becky?"

"The same thing about the woman in black, but added that she was motivated by jealousy."

"At least we have confirmed it was a woman," Jeff said.

"Assuming she is indeed talking about our shooter and not another woman dressed in black who may have killed her true love?" I said. "Shall we get back now? I've no wish to meet any of the other ghostly residents of this castle."

Constance meowed and we followed her down the stairs.

When we reached the gallery, I felt a buzz and Constance hissed. I saw movement on the lower floor and heard footsteps as someone ran away from us in the dark. I grabbed Constance to prevent her from following. In the distance we heard a door bang. It echoed for some time, around the space where the parties were held but it was not clear where the noise originated from.

"They've escaped, see if you can see them." I shouted to Jeff who dashed back to the turret to get a view from the top.

"I thought Jeff said he'd locked the door?" Lynn said taking a wriggling Constance from my arms.

"Let's wait for Jeff and get out of here," I said.

"I can't see anyone outside," he said a minute later, when he returned.

When we reached the front door, we found it was still locked.

"They must still be in here," Jeff said.

"We need to call the police, lovey."

"Remember they never found the gun," Jeff said.

"Maybe it was the shooter, coming back to collect the evidence they've hidden," I said.

"True, the castle is rumoured to have many hiding holes, plus secret tunnels," Lynn added.

Jeff unlocked the door and we went outside. I pulled my mobile phone out of my bag to make the call.

CHAPTER 10

I sighed as I watched the D.C.I. approach the van, he was wearing a waterproof jacket. I was expecting a uniformed officer, not Bad Cop Brad. I wound down the van's passenger window, it was now raining hard.

He growled at me as the rain dripped off his hood. "What are you doing here?" He gestured inside the van at us. I could see the head of his snake tattoo as he leaned forward. The D.C.I. had been an undercover cop early on in his career.

Constance hissed, she was not a fan of Brad.

"I run ghost hunts from here every week," Jeff called from the driver's seat. "You can double check with the castle administrators."

"So, you three were attempting to raise the dead in one of your so-called investigations?"

"As I understand it, you're not investigating the

shooting," I said crossing my arms. I'd done nothing wrong, and I wasn't going to allow him to bully me.

"It's part of on-going enquiries."

"I don't think this was anything to do with a gang. You're barking up the wrong tree. Conner was shot by a woman who was jealous."

"Of what?"

"Well, I don't know. Maybe of me?"

"So, it's true. You're in a relationship with Davies?"

"No, of course I'm not. But someone else may have thought I was."

"And they just happened to have a gun with them? At a party? People don't carry guns in Branden Bay. This was a planned killing. A hit on a crime lord, by a rival organised crime ring and you were nearly collateral damage and they're probably watching your every move now, thinking you're working for Davies. You're in danger and need to keep out of it and away from this place."

I shuddered. "You think I'm their next mark?"

He shook his head. "I'm not discussing the case with you. Just stay out of it."

The rain battered the van as a huge gust of wind blasted inland.

Brad steadied himself before continuing in a raised voice. "It's being dealt with by vice in Bristol. You're messing up the case with your interfering. Be at Branden Bay station at nine thirty tomorrow morning. We'll take a formal statement from the three of you."

"Aren't you going inside to search?" Lynn asked.

"Just leave. Now. It's none of your business what I'll be doing."

Constance growled from my lap.

"Really," Lynn said, clearly put out by his rude retort.

Jeff turned on the engine and we left, without bidding Brad goodbye.

THE FOLLOWING MORNING, our visit to the police station ate into my Saturday. Luckily the D.C.I. had not been present. We left the station at just before noon.

"What do you think after that, lovey?" Lynn asked as the three of us walked down the High Street.

I shrugged. "They were convincing, as far as the crime ring was concerned. They showed me a mug-shot of Spud, the goon who was up at the castle, who I identified as the guy who had threatened Connor."

"I saw it too," Jeff said. "Not that I noticed the guy on the night. I probably would have just thought he was a bouncer."

"Maybe the ghost is muddying the waters?" Lynn said. "The D.C.I. could be right, and it was a professional hit."

"Perhaps I should let them get on with it?" I said, suddenly feeling very tired of the whole thing.

"I'd feel a lot happier if you did. I worry about you," Lynn added.

H had called me first thing as well, and asked me to step back, no doubt prompted by Brad.

"I'm turning down here to the hut, lovey."

"I have to get milk," I said to Jeff.

"I need to get off to Iona's," he replied.

"You go ahead then." I said. "And thanks to both of you, I'm sorry I've dragged you into all of this."

"Nonsense, lovey. We're always here for you." Lynn gave me a hug.

After calling in to the grocery shop, I walked down the rest of the High Street with a bag containing the milk and a very large bar of chocolate. I was glad the rain had stopped, but it was still a bleak day. I passed the greasy spoon café, remembering the guy who had been watching us. *Who was he working for?* I asked myself. I stared at Connor's shop, where a van was parked and observed that refurbishments were well under way for the charity shop. Connor must have appointed them before he was shot. I hoped he would be able to witness the opening. I waved at Elena who was opening up Corelli's.

I rounded the corner of the High Street onto Beach Road as the wind blew at me. I pulled my coat closer and my hair billowed in the strong breeze, I wished I'd tied it back or worn a coat with a hood I could pull up. My hair was blowing all over my face, as I battled along Beach Road. I heard a vehicle accelerating and lifted my head towards the noise. I stopped in my tracks as a dark coloured car headed towards me, seemingly having lost control. I'd hesitated, but needed to move, to get out of the way. I was not sure which way to go. Making a decision, I scooted into the closed ice-cream parlour doorway, just a few doors down from my cafe and pressed myself up against the entrance, holding my breath and shutting my eyes.

There was no impact. As I reopened my eyes I saw the driver had regained control. I stepped forward onto the pavement, the car had already gone around the corner, having turned up the High Street.

"Idiot," I called out shaking my fist. "Some people."

A middle-aged man crossed the road from the promenade. "Are you okay?" he asked.

"Yes. But they could have at least stopped and apologised," I said as I stood panting.

"You're that Becky James, aren't you? How's your boyfriend? Is he out of hospital yet?"

I didn't reply and inwardly cursed the front page of The Gazette.

"We couldn't see what the driver looked like," he said. "But that guy took the number plate."

"What guy?" I asked.

He turned around and pointed to a man who hurried up the promenade. *Is that the man that's been watching me?* I thought.

"Did you see the driver of the car?" the passer-by asked.

I shook my head. "I was too busy avoiding it. They were probably drunk."

"Hopefully the guy who took down the number plate will report them."

After thanking the man for his concern, I composed myself and walked the rest of the way to my house. Maybe I had imagined the similarity between the guy walking away and the guy watching me and Connor. But forgave myself for being paranoid, after all I had been shot. I pushed the incident aside, I had more important things to worry about, than a drunk driver.

As I entered my house, Constance sashayed up to me. I was keeping her inside, with the weather being bad. I picked her up, realising I was no closer to finding the shooter. I'd told the officer who interviewed me up at the station, that I would leave it to the police and had agreed with him that it was likely to be gang related, considering Connor's reputation, but I still felt inside that it was a jealous woman, who wore black and had a gun.

I decided to relax, the café was closed and the house was empty. I ran myself a bath in the en suite bathroom. I filled it with bubbles and lay in the tub watching Constance as she jumped onto my bed and settled down to sleep. She was following me around the house, clearly sensing my unease. I had my phone on speaker, playing a selection of relaxing music and popped a couple of squares of chocolate into my mouth as I laid my head back.

Feeling much calmer, I emptied the bath then switched on the large shower to wash my hair.

As I got out, I looked down at my bruised legs. They were far from attractive and I was glad it was summer so no one would see them. I put on a new fluffy robe and made myself a sandwich for a late lunch and took it into the snug. I planned to watch films all day and then have an early night. Constance snuggled up beside me.

My mobile dinged with a text. It was from Izzy.

Martha has an exhibition this evening and a couple of people have cancelled. Will you be a darling and come and support her? Doors open at eight.

I groaned. It was the last thing I wanted to do. I sat staring at the screen as another text popped up from Izzy.

Only if you're well enough, sweetie.

I nodded, the perfect excuse. I began to text back that I was still not one hundred percent, when another text came through.

It's at The Glenthorne Hotel, in Bath.

Before common sense prevailed, I messaged right back.

I'll be there.

CHAPTER 11

"But Boss, we should come in with you," Jeff said as I got out of the van outside the hotel, set on Queen Square where the exhibition was being held.

I frowned at him and Iona, they weren't dressed for an art exhibition at a posh hotel. They looked like they were ready for a grungy punk band gig.

"We can't take Constance in with us, can we?" I said. "And I can't leave her in the van on her own."

"Iona can stay in the van with her, can't you, baby?"

She frowned, but then nodded in agreement.

Constance hissed. I doubted leaving her alone with Iona was a good idea and I did feel a tad guilty, as I'd dragged Jeff and Iona away from a planned cosy night in.

"No, I'll go in alone. I'll keep you updated via text."

"Parking is a nightmare around here," Jeff said. "I'll have to keep driving around."

"Thanks, Jeff. I really do appreciate it."

He nodded at me. "I know, and I'm always there for you, boss. I just wanted to make sure you're safe."

"Izzy will be there. It's fine." I waved them off as Jeff drove away. I'd already sussed out where Mr Angel's club called Ripples was, in case I decided to pass by later and had brought my disguise. It was only a couple of streets away.

As I entered the old Edwardian hotel, I followed the signs to the exhibition room and found Izzy standing just inside.

She smiled as I approached. "Darling, I'm so pleased you came. It means a lot to me. You're going to adore Martha's work."

"Okay," I said as I went further into the room, then stopped dead as I stared at the paintings. I'm the first to admit that I'm a bit ignorant when it comes to art, but I was sure that even Constance could do better.

"She calls herself an emotion-focussed impressionist," Izzy said.

I hadn't heard of the term before, but the painting in my vision looked like someone had had a food fight on canvass. Before I could stop myself, I turned to Izzy. "How does that work?" I said. "When she's doing your portrait?"

"Darling, I've enough realistic pictures of myself to

post daily on Insta for the rest of my life. I don't want something that looks like a photograph."

Martha approached us and Izzy held out her hand and clutched Martha's. "I want a portrait that's fresh and real. Earthy, vibrant and full of passion." She smiled at Martha, then turned back to me. "Martha paints what she feels when she channels the subject." She fluttered her eyelashes at Martha. "Darling, explain it to Becky."

Martha nodded at me and let go of Izzy's hand and gestured to the painting nearest us. "This one is called Supermarket Checkout."

"Nice," I said as I frowned at the splash of colours with brown running through the centre.

"It includes the essence of the environment, of the atmosphere, of the implicit emotions it coveys, to me. Not only as the observer, but as a part of the very fabric of that unique experience."

"Right," I said wondering what on earth she was on about.

"Isn't it amazing?" Izzy gushed. "Martha is simply a genius. When I look at it I can literally feel myself at the conveyor belt."

I raised my eyebrows, not so much surprised at the artwork, but at the concept that Izzy had actually been inside a supermarket.

"She's starting my portrait this week, I simply can't wait." She hooked her arm into Martha's.

"Izzy says you're interested in buying one of my pieces for your cafe?" Martha said.

"Um ..." I had to come up with an excuse. "I'm not sure if your work would be a little too cutting-edge for my traditional Victorian house."

"I thought you were getting rid of the antiques and modernising," Izzy said, opening her eyes at me so her lashes nearly touched her brows.

"Oh yeah," I said, feeling as if she'd sent me a memo, I had yet to read.

A woman called out in a European sounding accent. "Martha, what a spectacular display."

Martha slipped away.

Izzy put her arm in mine and led me away. "Why don't we have a look around and see if there's something which catches your eye."

As we walked to the back wall of the room I turned to Izzy. "It's not really my thing."

"I know that, darling." She huffed. "Try not to make it *too* obvious."

I looked at the price tag of the painting before me. "Three thousand quid?" I said a little louder than I meant to as my words echoed around the high ceilinged room.

Izzy gave a nervous laugh. "Shhh," she said as she looked behind to see whether Martha had heard.

Martha was now talking to a slim woman with shoulder length black hair.

I put my hand to my mouth. "It's the devil," I said gesturing towards them.

"Martha is not the devil. Are you feeling okay? Was it the shooting? Has it wrecked your grey matter?"

"No," I whispered. "That woman with Martha, she was dancing with Connor at the Halloween Ball. She's a fashion designer called Sofia Arbello."

"Yes, I do know Sofia, she's famous, sweetie. Everyone knows her."

"I haven't heard of her before, but she's definitely on my radar."

"Be careful. She lives in the same world as Connor. Let's follow her around and on the way, you can pick out one of these paintings. They aren't selling, so I'm keen to close on at least one of them."

"I hate to say it, but with the café being closed more than it is open, I'm living off my savings and don't have any flash cash for a three grand painting." I gestured at the *supermarket checkout* creation. "And even if I had the money, I couldn't hang that on my wall, it looks like a decorators dust sheet that's been used to clean out a donkey enclosure."

Issy pursed her lips. "Don't be unkind. Are you just uptight because your love life isn't working out?"

"I didn't mean to be rude. I'm just trying to explain what my eyes see when I look at it. I'm being honest – this type of art is not for me."

"I didn't mean for you to buy it and hang it. You'll

choose it and I'll buy it, pretending that you purchased it. I'll transfer the money to your account."

"Izzy. Don't you think that's a bit extreme. Maybe if Martha hasn't sold any paintings, they aren't the sort of thing people want to hang on their wall. You'll be encouraging her to fail."

"I thought you were here to support her." Her eyes filled with water.

I've really gone and done it now, I thought. "Hey, Izzy, I'm sorry. Look, let's start again. Take me around the paintings and I'll have a more open mind. I'm just rattled at the moment. I'm sorry."

I traipsed after Izzy as she explained every splash on every inch of canvass as I eyed the clothes designer. *Could she be the shooter?* I asked myself. She was about thirty and looked quite fit with defined calves. If it was the shooter up at the castle the previous evening, they had bolted at speed through the castle.

Martha approached us. "Sofia has bought Monday Menstruation," she said to Izzy smiling, seemingly thrilled that a famous face had made a purchase.

"That's amazing, darling. Well done." Izzy rubbed her arm and gave me a smug look.

I looked over to Sofia admiring her new piece of wall art, staring at the canvass which was ripped in places. I guessed that Martha must suffer with really bad P.M.S.

Sofia went over to the desk and handed over her payment card as she drunk from a glass of bubbly.

I chose the cheapest painting for Izzy to buy, which was a small oil painting, the size of an A4 sheet of paper, which looked like roadkill, and was simply entitled, 'Badger'.

Izzy seemed thrilled and it was a snip at nine hundred pounds. I paid on my credit card and Izzy transferred the money immediately to my bank account, via her banking app. It actually worked to my advantage as it helped my cash flow situation as the credit card bill would not have to be paid for another month.

Sofia kissed Martha on both cheeks, then left.

"I'm off now," I said quickly, eager to follow the fashion designer, but I didn't want admit that to Izzy. "Jeff and Iona are waiting with Constance in the van. They want to get back, Iona has a surprise for him, apparently."

"How sweet young love is," Izzy said.

I huffed to myself as I left, the only surprise in my love life was when my boyfriend actually turned up for a date. I wondered whether I'd see him the following day, as planned.

Once on the street, I spotted Sofia ahead of me, walking away from the square. I sped up and followed until she turned into the next street. I slipped into a dark shop doorway and pulled out a plastic bag, which held my short black wig and tinted glasses. I put the disguise on, still hearing Sofia's high stilettos clicking on the pavement. I adjusted my wig in the reflection of the shop window and then smoothed it down as I followed. I walked on the balls on my feet, so that my heels did not also make a sound. Sofia slowed and I stopped, pulling my phone out and texted Jeff to tell him I was in pursuit and to check my phone's G.P.S. tracker, so he could keep tabs on my location.

I put my tinted glasses on and thrust my phone back into my bag as Sofia sped up. After a couple of minutes, she stopped at a club with a bouncer outside standing in front of a red rope. She nodded at him and he let her pass.

I thought I heard someone behind me and turned my head. But I could see no-one there, probably because I was wearing dark glasses. Maybe I was imagining it, but that wasn't surprising, I was bound to have been sensitive, seeing as I'd been shot. My nerves were still rattled and I felt conspicuous outside in the street. I decided to follow her into the club. As I got closer, I noticed the name above the door in an antique style gold font, on a black background — Ripples.

I stopped dead realising this was the home ground of the Bath crime ring. And then I recognised the bouncer – Spud.

"Evening," he said nodding as I approached. He unclipped the rope and let me in.

I gulped and nodded back, he didn't seem to clock it was me as I walked inside. Music thumped in my chest as I entered the club. There were customers inside of all ages, ranging from students to older people, so I didn't look out of place. I made my way to the bar, still wearing my tinted glasses, wishing there was a mirror so I could check that my wig was in place.

At the bar, I was served immediately, even though there were others in the queue.

"What would you like?" the bartender asked.

I looked around to what other people were drinking and decided a bottle was a good bet.

"A Vodka Berry Spritz," I said naming the latest brand of alcopop I recognised on the shelf and had seen a few adverts for.

He passed the bottle over and I paid via contactless and picked up a straw, popping it into my bottle. I took a sip – it was rather delicious, but I told myself not to drink too much, I was on the last day of a course of antibiotics and had to have my wits about me.

I stepped away from the bar and looked around for Sofia. Finally, I found a great place to observe the dance floor and bar and stood with my back against a door which had *no entry* written on it. I went on tip toe as I spotted Sofia, she was waving at someone, but before I could see who it was, the door behind me opened. I gasped as someone grabbed my shoulders and clasped me in a vice-like grip, as I dropped the bottle of drink.

CHAPTER 12

"Hey," I shouted as I was dragged into a corridor. I tripped over and fell to the ground. "What's the big idea?" I felt the cool tiles against the skin of my bare legs, as I was dragged along the floor. The bruises I had forgotten about, were now painfully tender. "Stop."

"Shut it," the guy doing the dragging said. I recognised his voice and a hot flush covered my body as I registered that it was Spud. A vision of Mr Potato Head filled my mind. He opened a door and thrust me inside as if I was a bowling ball and I skidded along the floor not stopping until I slammed into a very large pair of smart brogues at the foot of a pair of long legs.

I sat up, still clutching my bag and adjusted my wig as I peered up at the wearer of the black shoes. I was in what looked like a control room, with many C.C.T.V screens. A middle-aged silver fox with a goatee beard, stared down at me.

"Becky James, I presume?" he said in a posh accent.

I picked up my glasses, which had fallen off at his feet, but did not put them back on. Clearly my disguise had been far from successful.

"I'm not impressed with your customer service," I said, doing my upmost to steady my voice.

"Next time you decide to disguise yourself, I suggest you tuck all of your flaming red hair into the wig, rather than wear it as a hat." He gave a chuckle which sent shivers of static up my neck, telling me this was one dangerous man.

I didn't want him to know I was scared, even though my heart thumped at full pelt. "I'm not impressed with the way you treat your new clients," I said gesturing at him with my fist.

He held out his hand and laughed.

I grabbed it as he hoisted me up until I was standing.

"Thank you," I said brushing myself down. "Now what do you want with me?" I asked in a clipped tone trying to adjust my wig, before giving up and pulling it off. I thrust it into my bag as my sore bruises made my eyes water.

"I want to know what you're doing here?" he asked. "Presumably you're spying on me?"

I turned around to see Spud, with his arms crossed blocking the door. Then turned back to the man. "I assume you're Damian Angel?" I was channelling my performing arts training. I'd spent three years training at university. We'd been told how to pull off a great performance, even if you had stage fright. And I needed to come across as cool as a cucumber juice on ice.

He nodded. "And you're Conner's latest lover."

I huffed. "I'm not in a relationship with Connor. But I'm not happy that he was shot, and that I was caught in the crossfire."

"So, I see," he said pointing to a copy of the gazette on his desk.

I scanned the C.C.T.V camera displays to see that one of them was paused on a still of me entering the club.

"Why are you here in Ripples?" he asked.

I didn't want to say I was following Sofia. "The police think you shot me. I'm not happy about that."

Mr Angel laughed. "So, you're taking on my firm. A little girl like you?" He smoothed his beard with his hand, in a similar way that I would pet my cat. "You've got some spunk, I give you that. Davies is lucky to have recruited you."

"I'm not on his books." I crossed my arms. "I just want to know why I was shot at."

"Look, honey, it was nothing to do with us."

"So why have you abducted me?"

"I want to know why you've brought the police here."

"What do you mean police?" I said.

"Him." He pointed to another C.C.T.V display which was frozen. "Who is he?"

I walked over to the screen. I recognised the guy, from the café in Branden Bay the day I went to the shop with Connor and Izzy."

"I'd like to know that too. Are you telling me he's police?"

"He looks like it, the way he followed you. He has copper written all over him." He turned back to me. "Are you wearing a wire?"

"No!"

"Spud."

Spud stepped forward.

"Hey, keep your hands off me! Look," I said lifting my top up as far as I could without showing my bra, to prove I was wire-free.

"Okay. Sit down," Mr Angel said, gesturing to a chair. "It's okay Spud, I'll take it from here."

Spud left and the door banged as it closed behind him.

I breathed out as I sat on the leather seat opposite Mr Angel's desk, like I'd been summoned to see a very scary headmaster. He pulled out a bottle of whisky and picked up some ice cubes with tongs and plonked them in two glasses methodically, before filling them.

"Here," he said offering me the glass. "Drink this. I can see you're nervous. I don't want to make trouble with you or Connor. The only message I wanted to convey via Spud, was for Davies not to run any betting shops on my patch. The previous owner, Eddie Fly had a betting shop here in Bath and Connor is now the owner. Fly was small fry, his operation could be tolerated but I can't have Davies working my patch."

I took the glass of amber liquid from him. "We're not sure Connor will make it."

"The filth have been sniffing around. They think it was us that shot him." He gestured to the screen. "I thought he was one of their undercover officers."

"I recognise him. He was watching Connor and me in Branden Bay. I think he's been following me for a couple of weeks." I thought back to the person dressed up as Frankenstein at the ball, and the guy I saw disappearing down the promenade after that car had lost control. "Maybe he is police?" I looked Angel in the eye. "But I told the police that I don't think it was a crime ring that shot us."

"You did?"

I nodded as I took a gulp from my glass then choked on it.

Mr Angel laughed.

"Sorry, it's not my usual choice of drink," I said, but I liked the way the liquid warmed me as it went on its journey to my stomach.

Angel looked up at the screen. "If that's not police, who is he?"

I shrugged my shoulders. "Could you give me a printout as it will help with my investigation?"

"You really are a private investigator?" He leaned back in his seat and eyed me.

"I guess I am, yes," I said.

He swung his chair around and took a screenshot of the guy who was at the bar.

As the printer churned out the picture, he turned back to face me. "I'd never take Davies out. There's no benefit to me if he's dead. We have an understanding. If the leader of a firm is taken out, trust me, it's an inside job. It always is, we have to be careful who we let into our circle. Your shooter will be closer to home, than me." He handed me the printout. "If that's not police, don't tell them you've been here. Do you understand?"

I nodded as I knocked back the last mouthful of the whisky, liking the way it calmed me and hoping it didn't act as a lethal cocktail with my medication.

"They're always on my back, looking for a way to pin any crime on my firm to take the operation down. But this is nothing to do with me."

"Can I go now?" I asked.

He stood up. "I'll show you out the back way. Do you want me to deal with that guy?" He pointed to the sheet of paper I held.

"No. Please. He's probably working for someone, and I won't know who, if you scare him off." *Or kill him,* I thought. "But I just wondered about one of your customers. Sofia Arbello?"

"She's a regular and lives close by." He looked back at his C.C.T.V. "Do you think she's involved?"

"I'm just looking at people who were connected to Connor and also attended the Halloween Ball that night."

"She's from our background. Her father has a firm in The East-end. He pumped a lot into her business and helped promote her shows."

"I see." As Izzy said, Sofia was clearly from the wrong side of the tracks, her father must be some kind of Spanish mafia man.

"Connor sponsored her fashion shows, I've been to them myself."

"You have?" I frowned, Mr Angel didn't look like he followed fashion, although to be fair, he was dressed in a stylish suit.

"And watch out for Connor." He shook his head. "He'll break your heart."

"I already said, we're not an item."

"If you say so," he said as he led me along the corridor to an exit, which opened out to a short service road. "Do you need a ride?"

I shook my head and lifted my phone. "I have one. And thanks," I said as I waved the printout at him.

I walked along the road with my legs shaking and called Jeff to come and pick me up.

As he drew up, I opened the van door and got in next to Iona. Constance immediately jumped onto my lap.

"How did it go, boss?" Jeff asked.

I didn't fancy going into the whole thing with Iona staring at me so eagerly. "I checked out Ripples club. I have a few things to be going on with." I stroked Constance's head. Bath was nearly an hour's drive from Branden Bay. "I hope Constance has been behaving herself?" I said.

"She's a really interesting cat," Iona said. "I have been wondering ..."

"Yes?' I asked.

"Do you think she's possessed?"

"Has she been swiping at you?" I asked. Wondering whether Constance had been channelling her evil streak.

"No, she's been fine, but I just noticed, the E.M.F meter always emits a higher change in the field when she's around."

"Well, she does appear to sense spirits," I said. "Although people have suggested, that she's just sensitive to my mood change, rather than the actual spirits themselves." I stroked her head. "But she really has got a big personality, haven't you?" I gave my cat a cuddle and she purred. "I need calming down, I'll put on some music." I leaned forward and turned on the radio as loud gothic punk blasted out. "What's this?"

"Just a station I like, sorry," Iona said as she changed the station.

"Excuse me for being unsociable, but I've found this evening a bit tiring, I'll probably sleep the journey." I laid my head back, while listening to Iona and Jeff discuss the possessed. They really were well suited.

CHAPTER 13

The following morning, I woke at eight after a restless night. Jeff had dropped me off at just before midnight, before zooming off with Iona to her place, for the surprise she had planned for him, which I didn't really want to dwell on.

It was already eleven when I finally dragged myself out of bed. I should have opened the café but had messaged Lynn the night before to say I was too tired. I really needed to slow down. I wasn't going to get better if I stayed out late and got thrown about by gangsters. I cuddled Constance as I looked out of the window at my back garden to see that it was sunny. The apple tree had shed most of its leaves and there were only a few brown ones left, clinging to the branches. On the floor were the last of the windfalls, turning to mulch and fading into the grass. The garden looked a little sparse without the lush green leaves of the spring and summer.

Constance followed me as I padded down the stairs in my slippers to the kitchen to make myself a coffee. I found Jeff at the kitchen table. He had a pained expression on his face and his hand cupped his ear.

"Are you okay?" I asked.

He nodded, but his face was flushed.

"What's up?" I asked.

He pulled his hand down to reveal a hooped earring in a very red earlobe.

Constance gave a pitiful meow.

"I don't remember seeing that?" I said. "Where did you get it done?"

"Iona did it last night. The earring was my surprise."

I shook my head. "You shouldn't have home piercings. It looks sore. You need some white spirit on that." I opened the cupboard and reached for my first aid box.

"Before she went to work, Iona said I have to twist it every few hours, but it feels like it's stuck." He shut his eyes. "I think I'm gonna puke. I hate needles."

"Then why did you have it done?"

"She said it would suit me."

I looked at the black t-shirt he was wearing with the logo of a band called *Pubic Scream*.

I sat next to Jeff and placed a hand on his forearm. "I spent many years in clothes that Marcus wanted me to wear. Having my hair up, just as he wanted it. Don't fall into the same trap. You have your own style. Stick to it. This outfit you're wearing makes you look like a gothic punk."

"It does?" He sat up with a grin. "That's the look that Iona said would suit me." He touched his hair. "I was thinking of dying my hair black and my beard purple."

"No way. You'd look ill with your complexion and your sandy hair colour is lovely, with the natural red tints."

He looked down. "Iona said I'm a ginger and she doesn't like it."

"Charming," I said stroking my vibrant red locks. "Look, just because your girlfriend dresses like she's at a funeral every day of the year, doesn't mean you have to match her look. Please, Jeff. I don't mean to sound like your mother here, but hang off from the whole Emo make-over. She needs to love you, for you, not some character she wants to turn you into." I sat up. "Anyway, I like your usual style."

"You do?"

"Yeah." I wouldn't have gone called it stylish, but Jeff was recognisable as he wore faded jeans, teamed with various superhero t-shirts. "It's good to have your own vibe," I said hoping I sounded on trend and convincing. "Now, what are we going to do about that ear?"

He touched his lobe and flinched. "It hurts but unless I keep it in, I'll never fit a stretcher in there."

"A stretcher? No, no and no," I said as I reached for the first aid box. I pulled out an antiseptic wipe. "Shut your eyes and take deep breaths." I undid the earring and whipped it out, then slapped an antiseptic wipe on the sore red lobe. "Hold that in place."

Jeff screamed. "That stings."

Constance jumped down from the table and sped straight out of the cat flap.

"As I thought, it's infected. The earring is out and it's staying out." I heard my voice echo around the kitchen. I was definitely turning into Jeff's mother.

Dannie walked in. "What's all the noise about?"

"Iona did a home-piercing on Jeff and it's infected – so I removed it." I picked the earring up with another antiseptic wipe.

"Yuck," Dannie said as she scrunched up her pretty face.

"Iona said it suited me, and now Becky has ruined it," Jeff said, trying to get Dannie on side.

"That girl is taking over your life," Dannie said. "You need to dump her."

I exhaled, feeling glad it wasn't just me that was not so keen on the girl. Although Dannie was rarely keen on anyone she met and was the type of person who had to warm up to new people. She'd only just warmed up to Jeff and he'd been living with us for months.

Jeff looked at us both as if in shock. "But she's the

sweetest person I've ever met. You don't know her that well." He put his head on one side. "If you two were a bit nicer to her then maybe she'd come here more, instead of me going to hers all the time. She's really kind and generous. And she collects dolls."

A picture came to my mind of Iona hugging Chucky.

"And I love her," he whined.

I looked at his sorrowful face and softened my voice. "Dannie and I are just worried. But yes, it's not up to us who you go out with." I laughed. "I know I'm acting like the disapproving parent."

"And I'm the scary sister," Dannie said. "Just ignore us, but don't bother with the piercings, and don't let her do a home-style tattoo either!"

Jeff remained quiet, and I wondered whether a tattoo was next on Iona's agenda.

"I'm going to call a meeting tomorrow night, so bring her over," I said reluctantly.

He nodded then mumbled to us about his Masters assignment, before sloping out of the room. He was studying quantum physics in Bristol, as well as his D.I.Y. store job, the ghost hunts and helping me. I was worried he might burn himself out and reminded myself to be a little less harsh on him.

Dannie and I chatted about Jeff's relationship for a bit, like worried parents. We decided to take a step back with our criticisms of Iona, otherwise we would push him away.

After my coffee, I went upstairs. Looking at the time I smiled. H was picking me up at twelve thirty and we were going to Carol's for lunch and then out on a date. I was taking a mental break from the case and decided to have an amazing time with my amazing boyfriend.

Fresh from my shower, I put on a pair of black jeans and a purple jumper. I smoothed my hair which cascaded over my shoulders and grabbed my bag as the doorbell chimed up the stairs. The rest of the house was quiet. Dannie had left for Bristol for some daytime drinking with Blue and Jeff was still in his room studying.

I opened the front door and H scooped me up for a hug as Constance meowed from the ground. The three of us walked to his car.

"So how's your case in Exeter going?" I asked him on the drive up.

"I've eliminated some of the suspects, but I've got no solid evidence to charge any of those that are left."

"I know you can do it, H. You're a brilliant detective."

"And I hope you've been keeping yourself to yourself?" he said.

"Yeah." I looked out of the window as we turned into his mother's road.

"Don't tell me about it. Just stay out of trouble," he said. "How's Connor?"

"The same. He's not getting any worse, though.

They do expect him to make a recovery, but they don't know whether there will be any lasting damage."

Carol opened the door as we arrived. "How are you, my love? Come in. You should have stayed here with me, I would have looked after you."

Constance sashayed into the house as if it was her home.

"I'm fine," I said. "Honestly, I was out last night in Bath."

"Bath?" H said. "Don't tell me you were snooping."

"Izzy invited me to Martha Pine's art exhibition."

H seemed to relax.

I didn't add that I'd also been to Ripples nightclub.

"Was it good?" he asked.

"Maybe?" I shrugged. "Modern art isn't my cup of tea. But she seemed to sell a couple."

"Well come in, the whole family is here." Carol ushered us in.

Inside I was greeted by H's Dad, Paul and his sister Rachel with her husband and three children. I felt warm inside as I entered the family environment. Carol went off to feed Constance a double helping of steamed fish as H and I set the dinner table.

After an amazing family dinner of salmon en croute and crunchy carrots, beans and a smooth mashed potato, we chatted, as H's twin nephews played with his childhood train set. Constance swiped at the model engines as they passed her and made us all laugh.

At four, we bade them farewell and left Constance sleeping in front of the Blake family fire. H took me up to Millar's Hotel to their panoramic bar with views across the bay. We looked out at the sunset, which was not the usual orange glow, with only a few shards of light breaking through the clouds, Sunset happened much earlier in the day now that autumn was making way for winter. H and I laughed together, and had a beautiful evening, where dead bodies and suspects were not on the discussion list. I wished so hard that he could move back to Branden Bay, and we could have more evenings like that, just the two of us.

When we got back to my house, having picked Constance up on the way, we walked through the door and I hesitated, I didn't want to spoil the evening, but I needed his help. He had access to information I wouldn't be able to get my hands on. I had transferred the picture of the guy who had followed me to the Ripples club, onto my computer. I'd removed all of the background, so there was no way H would know where the picture was taken and had reprinted it, with just a shot of the guy. "I have a favour to ask," I said sheepishly.

Constance slipped away.

"Anything," H said pulling me close.

I leaned to the side and grabbed the picture from my porch table. "This man, I need to know who he is. He might be police."

He stepped back and studied the photograph. “Where was this taken?” he asked.

“He’s been following me.”

“I said, where was it taken?”

“I can’t say.”

“Tell me.”

I shook my head. “He was staring at me in the High Street when I was with Connor. And I think I’ve seen him twice since. And there was a man at the ball dressed as Frankenstein. I think that was him. He’s following me.”

“This needs to go to Brad.”

“No, I promised.”

“Who? Davies?”

There was no way I was going to tell him it was actually Damien Angel. I remained silent.

“What is it about Connor?” H stepped towards me.

“What do you mean?”

“What’s the attraction? Women fall over themselves for him. And you?”

“I’m not attracted to him.”

He shook his head. “All I can see in my head, is you, that night up at the castle, in his arms. Staring into each other’s eyes – just before the shooter hit. I’ve been waking up at night in cold sweats.” He ran a hand through his hair. “I might have noticed the shooter, if I’d not been staring so hard at you.”

“Look, there’s nothing going on between me and Connor.”

"So why are you hell bent on finding who shot him? It's dangerous out there."

"They shot me too!"

"Are you being honest with yourself?"

"Yes. And no way do I want a romance with Connor." I looked at the man I adored, tall, with eyes dark, I wanted to tell him, there and then, that I loved him. But we were arguing. I wanted the first time I said it, to be special. Not like this. I sighed. We'd had an amazing evening, and I'd spoilt it.

He checked his phone. "I have to go." He looked at the piece of paper I'd passed him. "I shouldn't, but I'll see what I can do."

I pulled him close, but he did not hug me back. I knew he was hurt by the situation, but I didn't say any more. It would have to wait.

As he got in his car to drive back to his life in Exeter, my heart felt heavy as I shut my front door.

CHAPTER 14

Everyone arrived at my house for the meeting. I didn't open on Monday's anyway, but had spent the entire morning and afternoon, cleaning and baking for the following day. All of the Halloween decorations had been dusted and put away for the next year. Izzy prepared my A-frame and held a set of photographs we had collated together. I'd had to do battle with her before she agreed to print off a picture of Martha, but had pointed out that in our last case, even H had made it on the board. "It's just about building up a picture," I'd said to her.

There was the usual gang present. Annie, Izzy, Lynn, Dannie and Jeff who had brought a very eager Iona. I had also invited Tara. Marcus came with her, insisting he wanted to help. More, I'm sure, because he wanted to impress Tara than me! They were the last to arrive.

"How's Connor?" I asked as they entered the room.

"He's improving," Tara said as she waved at everyone before taking a seat at the tables, which I had pushed together in a boardroom style. "And Marcus has been so helpful."

"Well, you are paying me," he said.

"Of course," Tara said. "You can't take on any new clients if you're looking after my brother. So it's only right that he pays for your services."

"Looking after Connor?" I asked.

"Well. If I'm with Connor, Marcus is over at the gym and when I'm there, he sits with Connor at the hospital. The thing is, Connor's only conscious for short periods during the day, I don't want him waking up and thinking we've abandoned him. Especially with the police there. I don't trust them, I don't want them getting to him when he's drugged up and weeding information out of him. That lot don't always play by the book."

"I've been reading Connor thrillers, aloud," Marcus said. "It's difficult to know if he's following them, but it keeps me entertained."

Constance got out of her cat bed and jumped on the table, as if waiting for the meeting to start.

"Shall we kick off?" I said once everyone had a slice of the Blackberry and Orange cake I had made. It was a recipe that Carol had given me and after tasting it, I decided I would put it on the café menu.

Constance jumped from the table and sashayed

over to Izzy, who was now standing in front of the A-frame, which was set on top of one of the café tables.

Izzy stuck up a newspaper cutting of myself and Connor outside the soon-to-be charity shop. She wrote our names underneath.

"We have two victims," I said. "This time they're both alive."

"Thank goodness," Lynn added.

"We were all worried about you," Annie said.

"Connor and I were shot from a slim window situated in the right-hand turret of Branden Bay Castle. That evening, I saw the spirit of Lady Astrid of Cleve, who told me to beware of a woman wearing black, who is a killer."

Izzy stuck an exact typed transcription to the board.

"On our second visit to the castle she told me that the motive for the shooting was jealousy."

"So, it's someone who is so jealous of Connor giving you attention, they want to kill him?"

"My brother is a bit of a Casanova," Tara added with a sigh.

"We're not sure, who's jealous, or why. But let's go through the women he came into contact with, while at the castle." I turned back to the board. "First, we met Izzy and Martha."

Izzy smiled as she stuck a photo of herself and Martha at the art exhibition onto the board.

"Martha was wearing black," I added.

Izzy pursed her lips. "I've asked Martha and she said it was the first time she's come within yards of Connor Davies.

"But Becky said she gave him a really awful stare," Dannie said.

"She does not approve of him," Izzy said in a clipped tone. "And I hardly think she would be motivated by jealousy."

"Yes," Annie added. "I would not have thought Connor was her type."

Izzy looked at Tara and softened her tone. "Sorry, I know it's hard for you."

Tara shook her head. "My brother has behaved badly with women. I know that."

Marcus touched Tara's arm. "He didn't deserve to be shot, though. And neither did Becky."

"Lady Astrid's spirit didn't say what the shooter was jealous of, we're assuming it's to do with love. But we have to keep an open mind," I said.

Dannie continued to make notes on my laptop computer.

Izzy lifted the next picture so that I would move on. It was a snap of Connor's wedding.

"They look so in love," Lynn said, smiling at the picture of the happy couple.

I stared at the snap of Connor, in a heavily embroidered white suit gazing lovingly into Helen's eyes. She was dressed in a figure-hugging white lace floor-length dress with a blue bouquet of flowers. “Helen Davies, Connor’s wife.”

“They’ve been separated for two years,” Tara said. “Connor left Helen with their large house in Clifton and is reluctant to let her have any of the business.”

“Divorce settlements are often messy,” Lynn said.

“Especially when there are large parts of that business hidden from view,” Tara added with a sigh. “Helen knows she’s getting a slither of the pie, with a slice of what is declared and wants a real half.”

“Is she a jealous person?” Jeff asked as Iona gazed up at him.

“To an extent,” Tara said. “She left him because she couldn’t hack his infidelity. But I’ve spoken to her and she seems genuinely upset and keeps asking if she can visit.”

“She may be faking the concern,” Marcus said.

Tara nodded. “She’s been helpful though. She’s been over to the casino as she’s still legally part-owner, with the financial separation not yet finalised. Connor had transferred part of it into her name, to avoid tax. It didn’t go down too well with Connor when I told him she was there, but I can’t get away myself to oversee it.”

“Wes said she’s helped to calm the staff,” Annie said. “They’re really upset and seemed to feel comforted by her presence.”

Tara raised her eyebrows. “I guess I’d better get over there myself to check. She’s probably got her head in his books.”

"Next, we have a pink witch," I said.

"It's all I could get," Izzy said as she stuck up a cartoon picture of a pink witch.

"Clearly, she was not wearing black," I said. "But Connor spoke to her while I was there and the way she was looking at him, and then at me, told me she was suffering with intense jealousy." I turned to Tara. "Do you know who she was?"

"I haven't asked Connor yet about the woman dressed in pink. Why don't you come in tomorrow and ask him yourself?" Tara said.

"I'm opening up the café tomorrow, can I come in the evening?"

"Yes, six o'clock, will be ideal – just after he's eaten."

Izzy stuck a picture up of the next suspect.

"Sofia Arbello, the fashion designer," I said. "She was wearing black too. I understand that she has an on-off relationship with Connor and from what he said, it was definitely off at the Halloween Ball as I witnessed her slap him around the face."

"He supported her fashion shows and held a couple at the casino," Tara said. "But she always came across to me as a free spirit. Definitely not the settling down type. So I can't imagine her being jealous. My brother had probably insulted her, but to be honest, Sofia is a fiery character and she's still begging to see him, but Connor is not keen."

"I heard she has a ... domineering streak," Izzy said.

"And that is reflected in her work, of course. If you get my drift."

Lynn gave a small cough.

I frowned, no, I didn't get her drift. "I'd like to speak to her, if possible. But I will question Connor about her first. Sofia has connections to crime rings and has family in that world. Damien Angel told me her father has a firm in London."

"It may be best not to approach her," Annie said.

"If I need to, I'll be careful," I said.

"Is that it?" Dannie asked.

"Well, there's a man."

Izzy pinned up the picture of the guy from the C.C.T.V. at Ripples.

"This man has been following me," I said. "He spied on me and Connor when we were looking at the charity shop, there was a guy at the castle dressed as Frankenstein who I think was him. I saw him on the prom last week and he was spying on me at Ripples night club. I've given a copy of this picture to H, and he's checking him out. Although there has been a suggestion that he's police. But H messaged me to say he's pretty sure he is not part of any team working in that area. He'll see if he can find out more."

"I don't like this," Lynn said. "He could be the shooter, waiting to find you in a vulnerable position before he attacks."

"H told me not to investigate, of course," I said.

"As H has the picture, does this mean you have

reported this stalker officially?" Dannie said, looking out of the café windows as if checking to see if anyone was watching us.

I shook my head. "I'm keeping away from the local police, I'm on my last 'do not interfere' warning."

"So, what's next?" Marcus asked.

"I think the best way forward is for me to follow up with the cat charity fund raising."

"What the shop in the High Street?" Iona asked.

"Yes, I'm going to use that for my cover, saying I'm taking it forward, while Connor is in hospital. That way I can speak to everyone saying that I'm fund raising. I'm going to look into holding a charity event.

"Great idea," Lynn said.

"Darling you're a total genius," Izzy said.

"And I can take Constance with me," I said stroking my cat.

"Do you want to go up to the castle again?" Jeff asked.

"Yes, that's a great idea. We can take the full equipment," Iona said eagerly. "With the Ouija and the camera set up."

"No. I think I've enough to go on." I shuddered, that was the last thing I wanted to do.

I pointed to the C.C.T.V. screenshot. "I feel that guy is connected somehow. I'll go to the hospital tomorrow and see if Connor knows him. And speak to him about the fund raiser. Let's all pull together, organise a charity night and then invite all of our suspects."

"You could hold it at the castle?" Iona suggested.

I shuddered and Constance gave a low wailing meow.

"That's an amazing idea, baby," Jeff said. "I have the place booked out for every Friday night until two weeks before Christmas when the parties start!"

"It's ideal," Tara said. "Otherwise it could take a while to find a suitable venue, other than the casino."

They all congratulated Iona on her amazing idea, while she beamed with her blue eyes which did set off nicely against her jet black hair. Her pale face tinged pink. I had to hand it to her, it was a good idea and would hopefully flush out the shooter.

CHAPTER 15

I set off for the hospital at half five when the sun had already set. I left a very grumpy cat behind with Lynn. Keeping an eye on Constance was becoming a full-time task for her. Certainly, more of a job than looking after the café. Mrs Jessup had taken pity on us having elevenses and lunch but serving up an extra tea and sandwiches for my neighbour was not going to push me into profit. I knew I'd be better off closing for the winter but was reluctant to do so.

I carried a cake tin with a treat for Connor inside. As I walked along the dark promenade, I listened to the waves crashing on the shore. I saw a figure in the distance, underneath a streetlamp, it was a man in a leather jacket. I shuddered and squinted. Could it be the man that had been following me? A bus came into view as it rumbled down the seafront. I decided I would get onto it, rather than walk. I had to take care of myself. I would have asked Jeff to give me a lift, had he not been at Iona's. I felt a pang of annoyance. I stuck my hand out as I reached the bus stop, it was only a few stops to the hospital. As I got in, I looked out and saw the man hurrying away in the opposite direction. It was definitely him and I opened my bag and took a quick photo with my smartphone. *Who are you?* I thought. Hopefully Connor would have the answer.

"HE'S AWAKE," Tara said to me at the hospital as we passed the guard who sat outside Connor's room.

As I entered I saw that Connor had brushed his hair and was wearing a white t-shirt. I'd not seen him with bare arms before, and he clearly worked out. Not surprising, as his sister was a personal trainer. He stretched his hand out.

"Becky, I'm happy you're here. And I have to take the blame for you getting caught up in this. How's your arm?"

I approached him and placed the cake tin next to his bed, taking a seat.

"I'm off for my dinner," Tara said. "I'll be back in an hour."

It dawned on me that I was going to have to spend a whole hour with Connor. But I didn't blame Tara for taking a break.

"My arm's fine. How are you?" I asked. "I've brought you a ginger cake. I hope you like it."

"It'll be really tasty if you baked it for me. And I'm feeling stronger every day."

"You certainly look brighter."

"I want to get out of this place. I have money, I can pay for a nurse but they're keeping me in here."

I smiled. "I guess everyone wants to keep you out of mischief. They may be worried you will go after the shooter yourself."

"I would do, if I had any idea who did it," he said. "The thought that someone shot you. When I do find out who did it, they will pay." He began to wheeze.

I put a hand on his arm. "Stay calm."

"And there's police on the door," he said. "I've never been a fan of coppers, but that guy's not too bad. He plays cards with me."

"And lets you win?" I said with a smile.

"He does. I know his game, he wants to take me into his confidence to extract information. But I enjoy the cards." He laughed and then clutched his chest and laid his head back.

I realised that Connor was probably putting on a show for me. The guy was in serious pain. "Hey, take a couple of minutes. Don't do too much, too soon."

"That's what everyone keeps saying, but I need to get well to find out who did this to us."

"You have to stay where it's safe. I have a few questions to ask."

"Tara said you're investigating and that your café is

dead, so I asked her to transfer funds to your bank account."

"Connor, there's no need!"

He winced.

"Take five minutes," I said, as he laid back on the pillow. I pulled my phone from my bag and saw a notification from my banking app, that ten thousand pounds had been placed into my account. "Connor, that's too much money."

"It's nothing."

Although I was more worried about the origin of the money, rather than the amount. But I didn't have to accept it personally, it would come in very useful for organising the charity event.

Connor shut his eyes as a nurse came in, who reminded me of Lynn but with completely grey hair.

"Mr Davies, I told you to keep the oxygen on." She turned to me. "He has a punctured lung so don't keep him talking too long."

"I won't," I said. I realised I needed to get on with what I had to say soonish, before he was totally worn out.

The nurse checked the monitors and annotated a sheet on a clipboard at the end of his bed, then placed the oxygen pipe under Connors nostrils, before leaving the room.

Connor opened his eyes.

"We'll take it slowly," I said as I took a printed

picture of the man that had been following me, out of my bag. "Do you know this man?"

Connor frowned and shook his head. "No. Looks like police."

"He was watching us the day we went to the charity shop, he was at the Halloween ball, he was following me in Bath and today in Branden Bay."

"You went to Bath?"

I nodded. "I met Damien Angel."

"Becky, you need to be careful of that man."

"He was fine. I'm convinced it wasn't him. And he ran this picture off for me. He thought the guy was police, too. He sends his regards. I've asked H to check this guy out."

"Ah. Your boyfriend. I bet he's not pleased."

"No, he isn't"

"He's a lucky man to have such a brilliant and stunning woman."

I ignored the compliment. "So, do you know Martha Pine?"

"I've heard the name."

"She was with Isabella on the night of the Ball. She's an artist. Have you ever spoken to her before?"

"No."

"What about Helen, your ex-wife, do you think she could have done this?"

Connor sighed, then winced. "Who knows, our relationship was toxic at times, but I've never felt that she hated me."

"Is she a jealous person?"

He gave me a weak smile. "Unfortunately, I wasn't the model husband. Even though I should not say that to you." He stretched out his arm and took my hand. "I sometimes think, if I had you, I would change my ways."

I gave a nervous laugh, pulled my hand away and made some quick notes on my phone. "What about the woman dressed as a pink witch who is she?"

Connor groaned and then winced. "This is a nightmare, having to tell you all of this, you won't want to know me anymore."

"Come on, she looked green with envy and I was told the motive for murder was jealousy."

"By who?"

I put my phone down. "I've communicated with a spirit at the castle, who said that a woman in black was the murderer and she was jealous."

He raised his eyebrows. "This is interesting. You're a woman with a special gift. An angel walking on this earth."

"I don't know about that, but I need to find out about anyone who was wearing black and is jealous. Although the witch wasn't wearing black, she was clearly jealous, so I do need to know who she is."

He sighed. "I met her at my father's funeral, a couple of months ago and she's been stalking me ever since. I've tried to put her off, but she said she would talk to my wife and ruin the divorce."

I blinked as I watched him. This guy, a gangster, was being blackmailed by a young woman, not much taller than me. "So, she's blackmailing you?"

"Well, not for money. For my attention."

I was getting a picture that the pink witch was providing Connor with some interaction that he must enjoy, as what he was telling me, wasn't adding up.

"She's a nice enough girl," he said.

"And what's her name?"

"Willow Wilson."

"And now there's Sofia Arbello," I said.

He groaned. "She's fed up with me because Helen was making a noise about us, so I told her we had to stop her shows at the casino. She's had a cancellation in Germany and was trying to convince me to change my mind. Then when I refused, she said I cared more about money more than her. She also asked me to go back to Millar's with her and I turned her down."

"And that's when she slapped you?"

"Yes. She's a powerful seducer. I guess she couldn't handle the rejection."

"Could she have shot us?"

"She does have connections."

"Were you having a romance?"

"She wasn't my girlfriend."

I needed Connor to be straight with me. "So do you think, friends-with-benefits describes your relationship?"

He turned away, then back to me. "I'd have

dropped her for you," he said then closed his eyes and fell asleep.

I realised I'd worn him out. He slept for the rest of the hour while I spent some time trying to find Willow Wilson on social media. I could see nothing until finally I found her on Instagram. It was a new account she had opened in the summer. Included were a few shots at the Casino and one with Connor in his white suit and electric blue bowtie. Yep, I had the right woman.

Tara was a little later than she said, but I hadn't minded sitting with Connor, it had given me time to put my thoughts together. I smiled at her as she entered the room.

Connor woke up presumably at the sound of the door closing. "Becky, you're still here," he said.

"Yes, I was waiting for Tara to come back."

"Everyone's been great, including Marcus. He's reading me some fiction. I've never been one for novels, never had the time, but I'm enjoying it. Now could you do me a favour?"

I didn't nod my head. "What?" I asked.

"Could you see to my cats?"

"Connor, we're sorting them out for you," Tara said. "Helen has been feeding them, seeing as she was a part of their lives for a few years. And the cleaner still goes in. It's a long way for Becky to go."

"No, I want you to give them some love, Becky. Helen doesn't even like cats. She has a dog now. And my staff won't be petting them. Drop in when you can and show them some affection."

I didn't feel like I could say no, considering the guy had just put ten grand into my bank account. But it would be a great opportunity to snoop around his home. I smiled. "Of course, I will."

"Tara, give Becky a set of keys. And Becky, take your cat with you. See how they get on, for the future."

"Connor!" I laughed. "We're just friends." I stood up. "It's been nice seeing you. I'll keep you updated." Especially as I seemed to be on the payroll, I doubted that would go down very well with H, if he found out.

CHAPTER 16

On Friday, Jeff dropped me outside Connor's apartment, which was just down from the Casino at Bristol's harbour-side. I took Constance with me, as suggested, but was a little worried as to how she would react to the other cats.

"We're off shopping now," Jeff said. "Before the shops shut."

"Jeff's buying me a couple of new dolls," Iona said as she beamed at me.

"There's a great antique stall in St Nicholas' Market," Jeff said. "Then we're heading straight for the castle for a ghost hunt if you want to meet us? We're starting at seven as it's already dark by then. We'll be there for four hours, if you wanna meet us there?"

Constance hissed at them.

"I think me, and Constance will pass on that." I laughed.

Iona eyed Constance, no doubt still thinking my cat was possessed. *How ridiculous,* I thought. "I hope you find a bargain," I said as I got out.

After a walk along the harbour-side, I found the right apartment. Connor had the penthouse and I felt slightly excited to be meeting Betty the Bengal and Cindy the Siamese who he had referred to as his 'girls' in a follow up text to me. Connor, I was beginning to realise, was a man of many faces.

I passed the security guard and explained who I was before getting into the lift. I found the apartment on the top floor. I entered and kept Constance in my bag, I didn't want to create a cat fight if they did not get along.

I opened the door into a hallway. It was sleek with blue painted walls, divided by a white dado rail. Different mirrors were placed along the passageway. Clearly Connor liked to see his reflection.

As I wandered into his lounge, which had stunning views across the harbour, it appeared that Connor liked clean lines and minimalism. I found the cats on his sofa, curled up. They both lifted their heads. Constance meowed from the tote bag, but Connor's cats did not react at all. I pulled her out and she sniffed at the sofa then jumped onto it and settled down too. I sat next to Connor's cats and began to pet them, as he'd asked. Betty the Bengal purred as she looked up at me with her blue eyes. Cindy was less interested and gave me a little hiss. As I stroked Betty, I leaned back in the sofa, which I swear was the most comfortable I'd ever sat in and drifted off to sleep.

It was dark when I woke and I checked my phone to find it was a whole two hours later. I went to the kitchen for a glass of water to wake myself up before I left for home. The kitchen was beautiful, with dark blue cabinets and a granite worktop. I located the cat bowls, and they were filled with dried food. Someone had clearly been in before I'd arrived, filled them and seen to the litter tray. I decided to snoop around the rest of the apartment, I knew I should not, but could not help thinking I might find a clue.

Back in the hall I saw an open door, revealing Connor's office. My heart thumped as I walked in. Constance hissed behind me, having followed me and I felt a sudden fizzle of electricity and hesitated. A key turned in the front door lock.

I slipped further into the office with Constance behind me. I pushed the door to, then hid under the desk, holding my cat close to my chest. All I could hear was my beating heart and I hoped Constance would not meow. There was a scraping at the door. It opened.

"Cindy, what do you want in here?" I heard a woman's voice, which I recognised. It was Helen.

There wasn't any reason for me to hide, after all Connor had given me a key. But I didn't know how to explain why I was in his office, and I wished I'd not gone in there. Helen left the room and I stood up, planning to scoot across the hall to the bathroom and pretend I'd been in there all the time. After all, she would find my bag which I had left in the kitchen, but I stopped in my tracks when there was a buzz on the intercom. I returned to the table and crouched down as before.

"I've got a Mr Jones here to see you Mrs Davies," the security guard said.

"Thank you," Helen replied. "Send him up."

I stayed where I was, wondering who this Mr Jones was. I stroked Constance to calm her but felt fizzes in my hand. Helen had left the door ajar and Cindy the Siamese came around the table and hissed at us. Constance gave her a low growl in response.

I heard Helen open the front door.

"So, are we ready?" she said to this Mr Jones in the hallway.

"I'm nearly there."

"Thank goodness."

"I need to retrieve the gun, though."

"Are you going through the tunnel?"

"No, I've given up on that idea. I've booked myself on a ghost hunt. It'll be the perfect way in."

"But what if you're caught with the gun and it leads back to me?" she said.

"Helen, leave the details to me. If you have no information, they can question you as much as they like, you won't be able to provide them with any information and incriminate yourself. It's the best way. I can finalise it, you'll settle your divorce and we can be free of this."

I held my breath, not believing what I was hearing. It seemed to me, as if Helen and this man were in cahoots and he had shot Connor! It figured, considering Helen was wearing black at the ball and would rightfully be jealous of her husband with me, another woman." I shook as I remained under the table.

"I have to be in the casino now, to open the safe," Helen said. "But I don't want us to be seen leaving together by any of the staff on their way to work."

"You go first, then I'll wait for three minutes by the lift, before leaving."

"Okay," Helen said.

I waited until I heard the door being closed. I smoothly got out from under the table and tiptoed my way to the front door and peeped through the spy hole. As I expected, I saw the man in the leather jacket, who had been following me, standing by the lift. Now I had a name – Mr Jones.

My hand shook as I pulled my phone from my pocket, realising Jeff and Iona were in immense danger. I needed to warn them that this guy was on their ghost-hunt and he wasn't looking for a ghost, he was looking for a gun. I called, but Jeff did not pick up. I sent him a text.

Call me. I have found the shooter and he's going up to the castle now to get the gun! He's on your hunt and is called Mr Jones. He's the guy on the murder board that's been following me. About five ten, wearing a brown leather jacket. Get out of there.

Next, I called H, someone else that was not answering his phone.

Once out of the apartment block, with Constance stuffed into my bag, I hailed a cab. It wasn't going to be a cheap fare, but I had the funds from Connor and needed to get back to Branden Bay as soon as possible. I tried again to call Jeff, but he did not answer. Maybe he was already using it to look for spirits.

The taxi driver had been slow. Well, not slow exactly but he was adhering to all of the speed limits and driving methodically, and then we were caught behind a bus. And I didn't have the cash to pay him, and his card reader wasn't working so I had to stop at the cash point. I tried Jeff a couple of more times and wished I had Iona's number. Mr Jones would be well ahead of me.

When I finally reached the castle, I could see flash-lights from inside. Constance was hissing and wailing from my bag. I shuddered as I tried the front door, but it was locked. I didn't want to draw attention to myself by shouting for Jeff. I heard a voice in the distance and walked back, it seemed to be coming from the top of the turret.

The silence was shattered by a male scream as I saw someone fall to the ground their jacket flapped in the wind as they fell. I looked away as I heard a thump, followed by the sound of metal on the path.

There was silence and Constance jumped to the floor. Her fur bushing out as she let out a long and low meow.

I gingerly walked over to the body, close enough to see it was Mr Jones, laying on the ground with the gun that had landed, a couple of yards away.

I lifted my phone from my pocket and called 999.

Once I had placed the call and been through a series of questions, I ran to the front door and thumped on it. "Jeff, Help," I shouted. "Jeff."

I stepped back as the door was unlocked.

Jeff and his team of six ghost hunters came out.

Iona looked over at the body as she clutched what I guessed was her new doll and screamed. "No."

Jeff hugged her, covering her face. "Don't look, baby." He stared at the body. "He was on the hunt, he must have fallen."

"Didn't you get my text?" I said to him.

He checked his phone. "The service isn't great in there." As he said it, his phone buzzed with incoming messages.

"Didn't you recognise him?" I asked.

"I thought he looked a bit familiar," Iona said through a sob.

"He's the guy that was stalking me," I said.

Constance gave a low wailing meow.

'That's Becky James," I heard one of the guys whisper. "And her psychic cat."

A woman ghost-hunter stepped forward. "I'm a first aider."

I turned around. "There's no way he's alive." I said looking at his twisted remains as static raged through my body. "And we can't contaminate the crime scene. We need to be careful, if he was pushed, the killer must still be on site. Lock the door Jeff, now."

He put his mobile phone in his back pocket and locked the door.

"Do you think we should say a prayer or something?" Iona asked me.

I saw a glow just above the stalker's body. "Wait a minute, I see movement."

"What he's still alive?" asked a young guy.

I shook my head. "No, I can see his spirit." The glow of dots seemed to slowly join. As they came together, I saw the shape of a man depicted in a yellow light. "Mr Jones," I called out.

The E.M.F. meter bleeped in Iona's hand. She looked at me with her eyes wide and her jaw dropped. "Is he there?"

I turned back to the spirit. "Mr Jones." He did not turn around.

"Is he speaking?" Jeff asked.

I remained silent as I watched Mr Jones look around, as if confused.

"This is the best ghost hunt I've ever been on," another male ghost hunter said.

Jeff took his phone out of his pocket and lifted it to the corpse. “He’s there.”

I took a step forward. I wanted to know if he had shot me. The confession would satisfy me, even if I could never get the police to accept it.

The spirit scanned the area until he saw me. He stayed hovering in place. I moved forward.

“This is insane,” Jeff said staring at his phone.

“Mr Jones, did you shoot me?” I asked.

Constance moved in front of me. Fur on end, looking twice her usual size.

“My name is Larry Locke and she killed me. She pushed me, the evil witch.”

“Who is the witch?” I asked.

“You glow purple,” he said to me.

I looked at my hands. I couldn’t see any colour myself. “Larry, tell me the name of the person who killed you?”

“I’ve been watching you. She wants you dead. And she’s killed before.”

“Who?”

I put my hands up to my eyes, peering through my fingers at the slice of light appearing in the darkness. Like a static crack of lightening, which widened as I watched, mesmerised.

“What’s going on, Becky?” Jeff called out.

Larry looked behind him and I followed his gaze. The door to the spirit world was opening and with it came a burst of euphoria.

“Larry.” A woman stood in the doorway of light. She looked to be in her mid thirties and her arms were outstretched.

“Simone,” he called. He was sucked forward at speed, as if she’d breathed him in.

The door closed. All was quiet except for the emergency service sirens fast approaching.

I turned around and picked Constance up, holding her close as her coat returned to normal. The wind had fallen, and the collection of ghost-hunters watched me, open mouthed.

“He’s passed on,” I called back at them.

Jeff jogged over to me. “Was it him that shot you?” Jeff asked in a soft voice, so the others could not hear.

“No,” I said.

“Did he tell you who it was?”

I shook my head. “It was a woman, and she’s killed before.” I didn’t add that Larry’s spirit had said she wanted me dead. I was still shaking at the thought.

As Constance wailed in my arms, a police car sped into the carpark with an ambulance on its tail.

CHAPTER 17

"What were you doing at the castle?" Brad growled at me an hour later in the police interview room. He had come over from Bristol and was clearly unhappy.

"I was feeding Connor's cats when Helen Davies showed up, she spoke to Larry and he said he was going to Branden Bay Castle to get the gun."

"And instead of calling us, you waited until a man was dead to get in touch? And now we can't get a statement from him, or any sort of confession to shooting you because he's in the morgue."

I crossed my arms. "You never believe me when I give you information."

Brad lowered his voice and spoke steadily. "Overhearing someone in the flesh, saying they are going to retrieve a gun, is a bit different from you telling us some ghost told you a woman did it." He raised his voice. "Which they clearly didn't."

I licked my lips. "I heard him say the shooter was a woman."

"You spoke to him? When?" He sat back in his chair. "You said that he fell from the turret soon after you arrived."

I sighed. "This was after he died. I spoke to his spirit before he passed on."

Brad thumped his fist on the table. "You need to forget this nonsense. This is a serious matter. A man is dead. I only want to hear solid information and none of your hunches or so-called psychic sightings. You're making a mockery of our investigation." He pointed at me. "Do you know how disrespectful that is for the family?"

I gulped. I'd seen the guy mad before, but he was literally seething. I stared at him as his chest rose and fell as he took deeps breaths. But still, I knew he was wrong and that I was right. "Who was Larry?" I asked.

"None of your business."

"What are you going to do next?"

"Miss James, you're pushing my buttons," Brad said through gritted teeth. "We have the murder weapon and the potential owner in the morgue." Brad stood up. "Leave the enquiries to us."

"Have you spoken to Helen Davies?"

"I repeat. Leave it to us." He turned to the detective constable. "Wright."

D.C. Wright read out the time and stopped the recorder. She widened her eyes and shook her head at me as if to tell me to keep my mouth shut.

I ignored her as I watched Brad walk towards the door. "Larry was pushed and the killer was a woman, the same woman that shot me and Connor."

Brad turned back. "He was probably leaning over the top to shoot you and slipped. Get out of here. Now." He stormed out of the room.

Wright stood up. "Don't wind him up, Becky."

"Did you find anyone else at the castle?"

Wright shook her head. "Uniform are over there. But as you know, we don't expect to find anything as we believe we have found the shooter dead. So I'm not sure how thorough they will be with their search."

I shook my head. "Have you got Helen in?"

She stood up and nodded. "Brad is off to see her now. I pity her, with the mood he's in. Thanks for the information you have given us, and don't mind Brad. He's under a bit of pressure these days."

I smiled. "Is it impending fatherhood?"

Wright gave a small smile. "I couldn't possibly comment."

It appeared that maybe Bad Cop Brad was a lot more frightened of fatherhood, than he was of the criminal underworld.

As I reached the waiting room Jeff was there with a pale looking Iona, mind you she always looked pale. He had his arm around her. "How did it go?"

"Like usual. The D.C.I. hates me."

"You're a bit shaken up aren't you, baby," he said to Iona.

"Let's go home and then you can tell me all that happened up there," I said.

The three of us sat in the van and drove back in silence with Constance on my lap. We'd had to leave in the van. It had been a shock for both Jeff and Iona, to see Larry sprawled on the floor.

"I've not seen a dead body before," Iona whimpered, as she clutched her doll.

Jeff turned onto Beach Road.

"It's not nice," I added wishing I'd not seen a dead body before either, but I'd seen a couple. We continued the journey in silence.

Jeff parked outside our home and we got out of the van. The house was quiet. I assumed Dannie was in bed, unaware of what had happened.

In the Kitchen, Jeff had his arm around Iona as she nursed a cup of tea. Constance had gone outside, having been cooped up in the van for a while. I was steaming a fillet of salmon for her on the hob.

"So tell me what happened," I asked Jeff.

"We went up to the castle as usual, there were nine of us. Two guys from Bristol, two local women, a couple from Devon and the dead guy, who was a last minute booking who called himself Bob Jones."

"His real name is Larry Locke," I said. "Do you think any of the ghost-hunters, could be involved?"

Jeff shook his head. "The guys were a couple of students from Bristol Uni and the women know my mum. The couple seemed sound too. Not the sort to be mixed up with gangsters."

"So you locked the front door when you went in?"

He nodded.

"When I was at Helen's, she mentioned a tunnel to Larry. We need to find out where it is, as it's likely the killer uses it as her way in and out undetected."

"Lynn mentioned a tunnel, too," Jeff said. "I've already looked into it, although it sounds like the police think this case is over."

"They did find a man with a gun, and he was someone who had been following you," Iona said.

"I thought it was him earlier this evening, but not after what his spirit said to me."

"And what was that?" Iona asked.

"He said it was a woman who had killed before and that she was evil." I still didn't want to repeat that he had said the shooter wanted me dead. I wanted to push it out of my mind. "Tell me about the tunnel."

"There are at least two tunnels out of there, but the locations are kept secret," Jeff said. "Kids used to play in there until two died after the ceiling caved in. I heard they sealed it up. There are also priest holes, and the killer might have hidden inside and waited for the coast to be clear."

"Or hidden the gun in one of them," Iona added.

"Maybe Larry had worked that out and that's why

he went back there to pick it up. And it's possible the killer is hiding in a priest hole, right now. Waiting for the police to leave, so they can escape down the tunnel."

"Where does the tunnel come out?" Iona asked.

"The woods," Jeff said.

"Shall we go up?" she said.

"No," I said. "It's too dangerous." I'd not been to the woods since I was nearly murdered there and didn't fancy revisiting the place. "The tunnel must have been unblocked if the killer has been going in and out undetected. Maybe the police will put a guard on the door, to protect you in future hunts?"

"It doesn't matter," Iona shook her head. "They told Jeff he's banned from the castle."

"Oh no."

Constance came back through the cat flap and sniffed the air. I stood up and turned the hob off and removed her meal from the steamer to let her salmon cool enough, for her to eat.

Iona stroked Jeff's arm and gazed into his eyes. "And you've been doing so well with your ghost hunts, and all of them fully booked. I'm so proud of you."

"Are there any other haunted places you can hire out?" I said as I sat down.

"None as big or as popular," Jeff replied. "Especially after Izzy's article. Good job I didn't jack my job in, up at the D.I.Y. store."

"If you're convinced it wasn't Larry, can I help with the investigation?" Iona asked.

I really didn't want her involved, but looking at them all cozied up, I had to accept that she was now a part of Jeff's life.

"Sure," I said.

Jeff gave Iona a big hug. "I'm so pleased you two are finally going to be working together." He gave her a kiss on the lips.

I groaned inside as Constance meowed for her food. I stood up. "We need to find out where all of our suspects were, at the time of Larry's death. I'm going to feed Constance her salmon now."

Constance rubbed herself up against my legs and purred.

"You look tired, Iona." I said. "I'm sure you'll be wanting to get back home." I looked at Jeff and raised my eyebrows. There was no way they would be using my house as a love-nest. Especially when I was not using it that way myself!

"Oh, yeah. I'll drive you back, Iona."

"Oh, okay." She rose from her chair and smiled at me. "Thanks for including me, Becky."

As I went up to bed, I wondered whether my own romantic relationship would ever develop in the way Jeff's had. Would H and I ever spend more than a few hours together each week?

CHAPTER 18

I stroked Constance as I sat in the snug, waiting for Tara and Helen to arrive. H wasn't able to visit and I felt a little down, wishing I could share some time with him. I stared at the murder board. Brad had told me not to go anywhere near the hospital, so I had asked Tara to come to me. Although, I knew Brad could not order me where not to go, it was a free country and I had done nothing wrong, but I thought I would let the dust settle. When H had called that morning to apologise that he could not take the day off, he also asked me to steer clear of Connor and leave it to the police to follow their enquiries, no doubt prompted by Brad. The police seemed certain that Larry had been the shooter but he said he could not elaborate.

When they had arrived, I showed Tara and Helen into the snug. It was a chilly day and the snug was much easier to heat. I'd lit the fire and the logs were glowing. Constance positioned herself on the rug in front of the fire guard. I glanced over at my murder board. I needed answers.

Helen sat down and wiped her red puffy eyes. "I should have contacted the police sooner, then Larry would still be alive. There's no way he would have jumped off that turret. He was pushed."

"I'll pour tea," I said leaning forward to the coffee table as Helen began to cry. I cut her a slice of apricot and almond cake, hoping that would comfort her.

"The police have been giving Helen a tough grilling," Tara said. "They've only just let her leave."

"They're convinced that I hired Larry as a hit man because I was paying him as a P.I. it's not looking good for my defence. Luckily for me I have a good lawyer, otherwise I might be behind bars."

"Were you having a romance with Larry?" I asked, wanting to get straight to the matter.

"We were seeing each other but nothing serious. I didn't want it to develop until I had settled my divorce. And Larry was a widower, I wasn't sure he was ready for another relationship. I feared Connor would have used any male friendship against me in the divorce. Especially as I've known Larry for years."

Tara nodded. "He definitely would have. Let's face it, both of you have been pulling everything out as ammunition."

"So, who was Larry?" I asked.

"We met at school and used to go out." Helen smiled. "He was my childhood sweetheart. He went on to be a policeman and recently a P.I."

"So you hired him to help with the divorce case?"

Helen nodded. "And he said that while he was tailing Connor, he saw someone following you and ultimately, he thought that person was the one that had shot at you. And was then convinced of that when they tried to run you over."

I put my hand to my neck. "I thought that was just a drunk driver."

"So, someone did try to mow you down?" Tara asked.

I gave a silent nod, feeling my heartbeat quicken.

Constance rose from the rug and jumped on my lap.

"A passer-by said that a guy took the number plate, so presumably that was Larry and he found out who it was. I take it he didn't tell you the name of the shooter?"

"No," Helen said. "He had a contact in the force who gave him information, but this wasn't someone locally. He told me nothing, to protect me."

I accepted that as the truth, it fitted with what I had overheard them discussing when I was at Connor's apartment.

"Larry wanted no connection between me and the shooter, otherwise I might have been implicated. I clearly had the most obvious motive for wanting

Connor gone. But now, I'm in the frame anyway." She wiped her nose. "Larry was such a lovely man. Okay there were no fireworks, but he was safe and kind and as you can imagine, after Connor, excitement was the last thing I wanted." She gave a small laugh. "You'll discover that for yourself."

"I'm not in a relationship with Connor," I said.

She raised her eyebrows.

"I'm seeing a policeman." I stroked Constance's back as she tried to get comfortable on my lap.

"Larry should have just told the police, and not put himself in jeopardy," Tara said.

"The shooter was probably up at the castle trying to retrieve the gun at the same time Larry was looking for it. I wonder if he had found out where the priest holes were?" I said.

Helen sighed. "He probably would have stayed there all night looking for it. He had such a point to prove. Now I have been dropped well and truly in it."

"The police can't pin anything on you," Tara said. "You were no-where near the castle when Larry died. And you'll be pictured all over the casino's C.C.T.V."

"Tara, can I please now visit Connor?" Helen asked. "I want to explain to him what happened with Larry, before he hears it second hand."

Tara nodded. "You might have better luck in coming to an amicable agreement while he's in a melancholy mood. But I won't allow him to sign anything, until he is one hundred percent. I also need help sitting with him because my business is suffering."

"I'll visit him, when we're done here." Helen smiled at Tara. "I still love your brother. I genuinely wanted to find out who did this to him. And now ... poor Larry is dead." She gestured to me. "Anything you can do. I'll pay you."

"I've already transferred her some money," Tara said.

"But you can help," I said. "As you probably know, before we were shot, Connor was setting up a charity shop in Branden Bay High Street."

"He's obsessed with cats," Helen said.

Constance purred loudly.

"I'm planning on holding a charity night as a cover for my investigation and will invite all of the suspects."

"That sounds dangerous," Helen said. "Considering whoever it is has killed."

I nodded. "I'm hoping that during the process of inviting them face to face, I'll find out who the killer is before the actual event. If not, then yes, I will be somewhat of a pawn and hope that everyone around me will protect me, as we flush the killer out. At least they no longer have the gun."

"I wonder why they threw it?" Helen said.

"They probably wanted to frame Larry," I said.

"It certainly seems to have worked as far as the police are concerned," Tara added.

"And it would have worked. If I wasn't there. Jeff

and the other ghost-hunters would have just come outside later, to find his body on the floor with the weapon, which no doubt will turn out to be the one used to shoot Connor."

"I guess the real shooter used the tunnels," Helen said. "I knew that Larry had got hold of the castle plans."

"It's likely," I said. "We need to find them. To work out the escape route. But first, we need to start planning the charity event." I walked over to the murder board and dragged it across the room.

Helen studied the board and smiled at her wedding photograph. "We had the best day."

"I need all of these people invited. Do you know them?"

"Martha Pine? I saw her at the casino a few times. I didn't realise she knew Connor, though."

I hesitated, that wasn't what I was expecting, especially as Izzy was quite sure she had not been near Connor before.

"Really? She went to the casino?"

"Yes, I don't remember her at the tables, but I definitely remember her at the bar. I'm an art fan."

"Connor said he'd never met her before."

Helen smiled. "Martha isn't the sort of woman to catch his eye."

My heart began to thud. "I'll question her on it when I invite her to the charity do."

Helen pointed to the picture of Sofia. "The love-buddy. He knew her well before me and seemed to think it perfectly normal to carry on with their liaisons, even though he had a ring on his finger." She sighed.

"It must have been hard for you," I said.

"That man broke my heart constantly. I hated it, whenever she announced a show in town."

"And what about Willow Wilson?"

Helen frowned. "That's the stalker. Larry had all the details on her and logs of her movements. Connor thought I didn't know about all of these women. But I did. It was just a case of finding out which of them he was seeing before we split up and to show what type of man he was, running relationships alongside each other."

"Where did Larry keep all of this information?"

"At his office."

"No doubt the police have raided it now."

Helen frowned. "They didn't ask me if he had an office. I'm not sure they know where it is. Larry didn't publicise the location. He always met clients in public places."

"Can you take me there?" I asked. "It's worth a look."

Helen nodded. "It's this side of Bristol – at an allotment in Ashley Vale, it's near the railway line. I have a key for the shed containing his papers. We used to meet over there." She smiled. "We spent some lovely afternoons together, reminiscing. He was a great friend and good with veg." She blinked away a tear. "But anyway, you could help me collect the papers as no doubt they will help with my defence."

I saw Tara and Helen out and arranged to meet them at the allotment after they had been to the hospital. I called Jeff, guessing he was on his way back from work.

"Hi," I said as he answered the phone.

"Is everything okay?" he asked.

I heard Iona giggle in the background and Jeff was not driving, so presumed he was at her place.

"I thought you were at work today?" I said.

"I had a lie-in and missed the start of my shift. I wasn't feeling too good."

I could just imagine what sort of lie-in he'd had. "You'll get the sack at this rate."

He remained silent and I guessed I had my maternal voice on again. I took a deep breath. It was his life.

"Who is it?" I heard Iona ask.

"Are you feeling well enough to take me to Bristol in a couple of hours?"

"Er." He paused and I could hear whispering. "Yeah, for how long?"

"I'm just checking out Larry's office. I don't think the police know about it, so we're getting a first look."

"Where is it?" he asked.

"Bristol, somewhere," I said, not wanting him to pass the details to Iona in case she showed up.

"Okay, yes."

"It's probably best if you come back now, so I can go over where we are with the case," I said.

I heard Iona in the background. "Can I come?"

"We're bringing Tara back from Bristol, so there won't be enough room for all of us in the van," I added.

"Iona could drive?" Jeff said.

"No," I said. "Get here as quick as you can." I ended the call before he could ask any further questions. Truth was, I just wanted to spend some time alone with Jeff, without Iona in tow.

CHAPTER 19

Jeff looked scruffy with bags under his eyes, when he showed up, so I told him to shower and change. I updated him on the case as he drove us up to Bristol. He seemed to re-focus. I guess it was the first time he'd been in love and was totally smitten. I guess it was quite sweet.

After half an hour, the sat nav app on my phone told us we had arrived at our destination. We parked up at the field and as I got out, I thought how peaceful it was. As no-one was around, I let Constance jump out of my bag. She sniffed around the floor as her fur ruffled in the breeze and I pulled my coat close to myself. The air smelled fresh, apart from the feint smell of burned wood.

"What a nice place," I said, looking at the collection of plots.

"Do you know where his actual allotment is?" Jeff asked.

"No. We'll have to wait here for Helen and Tara. They won't be long."

They soon arrived in Helen's car which was a sleek white BMW cabriolet and I scooped Constance into my arms as Helen parked up.

"This is Jeff," I said as she got out.

Helen nodded to him. "Hello there, I recognise you from the newspaper reports. Come this way."

She walked ahead of us as we passed the various allotments. Then she turned the corner and stopped abruptly, pointing ahead.

Constance hissed as I held her.

Before us was a scorched allotment.

"It's gone," Helen said. "The shed. It's been totally burned to the ground."

"Someone came out and torched it this morning,"

We turned to the sound of the voice.

An elderly man leaned on his spade. "The fire brigade were too late. They said it was arson for it to burn like that, when we've been having this bad weather. Unlikely to go up on its own, they said. Told us to be vigilant, kids these days have nothing better to do. They asked me if I'd seen the little beggars, but I seen nothing. Place ain't so popular this time of year, folks usually come twelve to three, not early in the morning." He nodded at the scorched wet patch. "Larry's gonna be right fed up."

Constance gave a low meow.

We all looked at the guy, none of us wanted to tell him Larry had died. So we didn't.

As we about turned, my heart dropped. It had been our biggest lead. "I guess we're back to square one."

"Not really," Jeff said. "Now we know we have to find out where each of the suspects were at the time of Larry's death and this morning."

I smiled at Jeff. I was glad he was back with me, putting a positive slant on things. Mind you his positivity could be due to the fact that he had spent the entire morning at Iona's.

I turned to Helen when we returned to the carpark. "Is there anything he told you? Anything at all?"

She shook her head. "We kept communication to a minimum."

"How did he come to be a P.I.?"

"Larry got kicked out of the police on a disciplinary. He had a point to prove."

"Probably another reason he was keeping the details quiet, so he could take the glory," Tara said.

"Indeed. He dreamed of a front-page spread, like the ones about you, Becky. Showing him as a great P.I. to kick start his career. But it just got him killed."

"The killer must have found out where his office was. So who told her?"

"As far as I know, other than me, no-one knew where it was."

"The killer either clocked him watching her, and

followed him back here. Or he told her up at the turret, if she had a gun pointed at him. We'd better set this charity event up as soon as possible." I turned to Helen. "Can you book it out? Jeff has been banned from doing ghost hunts."

She nodded. "I'll call the castle administrators and ask Millar's if they want to get involved."

"I've a booking there in just under two weeks, if that isn't too soon?" Jeff said.

"The sooner the better," I said.

We bade Helen farewell, she was on her way to the casino. Tara got into the van with us and Constance settled on her lap.

"We need to invite, Martha, Sofia and Willow," I said.

"So, we have three suspects?"

"Of course, we can't rule out Helen."

"You don't really think she did it?" Tara asked.

"In this game, no one is really struck off the suspect list until the killer is found."

"Or they die," Jeff added.

"Poor Larry," I said. "I'll try to find out from H whether the police have any details from his mobile phone. He might have taken some photos as part of his surveillance. He certainly took a picture of Connor and me."

"It would be great to get a hold of that," Jeff said.

I nodded. "We need a meeting to decide how we're going to tackle this."

"How are you going to deal with the Martha issue, considering she's close to Izzy?"

I puffed out. "We'll have to tread very carefully."

We dropped Tara at the hospital, as she wanted to see Connor and update him on our progress.

As we walked into the house, Jeff stopped and faced me. "When are we going to have our next meeting?"

"Tomorrow night."

"Can Iona come?" he asked.

I took a deep breath. "Okay."

"Thank you so much." He gave me a hug.

I went up to my room feeling weary. I climbed into bed and fell asleep with Constance at my feet. I always felt safer with her there.

It was a restless sleep, full of dreams. In one I found myself in woods. I hated the woods. In the middle of the woods was a hut. I saw Lady Astrid, pointing to it. I tossed and turned trying to wake myself up, as static buzzed through my body.

I opened my eyes, but the buzzing continued.

Constance stood at the end of the bed, her coat fully bushed out, and let out a sorrowful meow, which made me jump.

Help, I head a scream inside my head, realising who the voice belonged to.

I got out of bed and stepped into the middle of the room. "Is that Lady Astrid of Cleve?" I called into the darkness. "Is that you?"

She wants to own me, the voice said.

I spun around, not knowing what direction the voice was coming from.

She has killed, the woman of the wood. Help me!

I blinked and rubbed my eyes. My hand shook as I put my bedside lamp on. There was no-one in the room. Was it a dream? I thought so, but the static filling my hands told me it had been real spiritual contact. Constance's fur remained bushed out, as she hissed. Was my cat just reacting to my emotions? Or was Lady Astrid in my house? I needed help.

"Jeff," I called out and banged on the wall between our rooms. "Can you come here? I think I've just seen something."

But no reply came. Because he wasn't there.

THE FOLLOWING day I prepared for the meeting while Dannie and Jeff were at college and Uni. The cafe was closed on Mondays. After everyone had arrived, we had a tasty meal of a huge cottage pie with a cheesy mash top, which I served with baked beans and salad. There were so many of us, beans were the easiest option. Jeff was in high spirits, with Iona sitting next to him. She was all smiles, but I was miffed that he had not been there the night before, when I had heard the wails of Lady Astrid. I was having difficulty shaking off my grumpy mood. If Jeff had been there, he could have confirmed whether the spirit was there with his equipment, or if it was just a dream.

As Dannie and Jeff collected the plates, Constance hissed at Iona and Lynn gave me a look, as if it was my fault. I went to the kitchen to fetch dessert and Lynn followed.

"What's up with you?"

"I needed Jeff last night and he was at Iona's, again."

"They're in love. You need to relax. I can see this is all getting on top of you."

Constance came in and meowed.

"And you're unsettling the cat. She's sensitive to your emotions."

"Another thing," I said putting my hands on my hips. "Iona asked whether Constance is possessed."

Constance gave a grumpy meow.

Lynn looked at my cat. "I've often wondered that myself," she said with a laugh.

I scowled at her.

Lynn put a hand on my lower arm. "Come on. Lighten up."

"Nobody understands," I said feeling a tear sting my eye.

Lynn gave me a hug. "I'm sorry, lovey. Come on let's get on with this meeting. I'm sure once we've talked it all through you'll feel better. You're under a lot of pressure."

Lynn helped me carry in a dessert of chocolate

trifle, with lashings of cream and once we had polished it off, I called the meeting to order.

Izzy stood at the A-frame and put a red cross through Larry's picture and then sat down. It went quiet, as if we were giving him a moment of silence.

I stood up and approached the A-frame, feeling a lot stronger.

Constance rubbed against my legs and stood beside me.

"Our suspects have remained the same," I said. "Apart from poor Larry. What we intend to do, is to arrange a charity event up at the castle and invite everyone on this list. It'll be a nice thing to do, anyway."

Izzy nodded. "Martha is innocent, of course, so we only have two suspects. But I'm sure she'll want to be involved. I can persuade her to donate a painting for auction." She turned to me. "I'm doing a dinner for her this Thursday. I wanted to get you and Annie over. H hopes he can come, as he missed our meal at Annie's and didn't manage to get here last weekend."

I smiled.

"I want to introduce you to her properly and you can cross her off your murder board," she pouted.

Annie nodded. "How lovely."

I agreed, it would be an ideal opportunity to question Martha, but kept that to myself.

"As we're on the subject of Martha, where was she on Friday night?" Iona asked Izzy.

Izzy stared at Iona. "Painting."

"Where?"

"At my place."

"Oh," I said, This was going to be easy. I could strike her off the suspect list. "So she was with you all night?"

Izzy remained silent.

"Izzy?" I asked.

"I was in Bristol catching up with Madeline Shah, I stayed at her place."

"So you weren't there in the morning either?"

"It's not Martha," Izzy said crossing her arms. "You need to question Sofia and check on her whereabouts. She clearly has a real connection to Connor, unlike Martha, who doesn't even know the guy."

"I take it, as you're a model, Sofia knows who you are?" I said.

"Of course," Izzy said.

Annie laughed. "Everyone knows who Izzy is. Maybe you could pretend you're interested in modelling for her?"

"No way." She ran a hand through her bob. "I'm through with that and if someone was there with a camera, I would certainly not be looking my best in one of her creations." She moved a hair from her forehead. "I'd end up on one of those 'where are they now?' websites with me looking haggard."

I laughed. "You're hardly haggard Izzy, you're only twenty-seven. And it doesn't mean we can't go and discuss it with her? Can't you pretend you're interested?"

Izzy sighed. "Okay darling, if it stops you harassing Martha. I'll pretend, but I'm not doing it."

"Either way, can you set up a meeting with her? I'll be asking her if she would do a mini-fashion show at the castle for the charity event."

Lynn frowned. "Do you think that's appropriate?"

"Why not?" I asked.

"I love her stuff," Iona said, then blushed as she looked at Jeff. The red showed up a lot on her pale face.

"It's a solid way of getting her back to the castle," Jeff said eagerly.

"Will it be adults only?" Annie asked.

"Of course, we're not going to invite families to an event to which we're luring a killer," I said wondering why my team were asking such questions.

"What about the pink witch? Who's inviting her?" Dannie asked.

"I need to question Connor further about Willow. I'm going in to see him after work tomorrow. And then I'll check her out."

"I'll come with you," Jeff said.

"Me, too," Iona added. "I could go under cover."

I groaned inside. "Thanks. I'll let you know once I've gained more information about her. The killer has to be someone relatively fit, due to the fact that they have run through the castle and up and down the turret. We need to find out where the tunnels are in the castle, as it's likely to be how the killer has gained access and escaped undetected."

"I've a friend who works up at the library," Lynn said. "I'll see if I can get hold of the castle plans."

"That would be great." I smiled at Lynn. "I also had something else happen last night."

"Go on," Izzy said.

"I had a dream, which may not have been a dream."

Dannie looked up and groaned. "Not another ghost in this house?"

"I heard Lady Astrid of Cleve and she was calling for help. And said that someone wanted to own her. Someone who has killed before, the woman of the wood."

"If it was spiritual contact, it sounds like the killer is definitely coming in through the tunnel, if the woods are mentioned," Lynn said.

"It might be something to do with trees," Iona said eagerly.

"Like what?" I asked.

"Willow is the name of a tree," Iona said.

"Well thought of, baby," Jeff said gazing at her.

"Maybe," I said wondering why hadn't I thought of that?

Constance growled by my side and I realised I really did need to chill out as we brought the meeting to a close.

CHAPTER 20

The following evening, I arrived at Connor's hospital room and looked through the door's window. Marcus was inside reading him a book. Connor appeared animated, so I stood with the policeman outside and waited.

"You're that psychic aren't you?" he said.

I nodded. "How is it going? Have you seen any suspicious characters lurking around here?"

He shook his head. "None more dodgy than the guy in there. But I like the man. Not gonna lie, he's great company. But then you have to have the chat, in his game."

"I hear you've been playing cards with him."

"He plays his close to his chest," he said.

The guy looked like he genuinely liked Connor. The force better be careful, otherwise they would be losing him to the casino at this rate. I had found out that one of the reason's Connor had such loyal staff was that he paid well – really well.

I looked through the window again and Marcus put the book down. I knocked on the door, then opened it.

Connor smiled. "Becky, what a lovely surprise."

"I've just popped in to ask a few questions," I said.

Marcus stood up. "I need to get a drink, reading aloud is thirsty work."

When Marcus had left the room I sat in the vacated seat, beside the bed. "You're not going to like this, but I need to know everything about Willow Wilson, the pink witch."

"I thought you said you were told that it was a woman wearing black that shot me?" he said.

"I know – I just need to eliminate her, completely."

Connor sighed. "All these women out to kill me."

"Only one is the killer. So you met her at your father's funeral. Did she know your dad?"

"No."

"What was she doing there?"

"This is embarrassing. Can you not leave it until you have discounted the others?"

"I don't need the finer details. Where does she work?"

He picked up his water and took a sip. "For Foster and Blythe."

"And where are they situated?"

"On the outskirts of Branden Bay, close to the crematorium."

"What's their line of business?"

"They're an undertaker."

"Right. She works at a funeral home which dealt with your father's burial?"

"He was cremated."

"Is there anything else I need to know about her?"

"She's a bit obsessed with me."

"Okay, I've heard a couple of people refer to her as your stalker."

"I wish you were obsessed with me," he said, ignoring my comment.

"We're setting up a charity event. I take it you want the proceeds to go to Save the Cats?" I said changing the subject. I had the information I wanted and didn't need to know any more.

My next step was to contact Willow and invite her to the charity night. But before that, Izzy had fixed up a meeting with Sofia and I was going along too.

Izzy had arranged for us to be taken to Bath in a limousine to meet Sofia. She said she simply could not turn up at her house in a cab. I'd not mentioned that Jeff could have given us a lift in the van. She'd never before accepted a lift with him.

We drew up at Sofia's house, set on a terraced crescent, opposite a railed green. Outside were an array of pots with evergreen bushes in. Constance hopped in my bag and the chauffeur opened the doors for us.

I pulled my coat to me as I stepped out of the car. It seemed a couple of degrees colder in Bath than in Branden Bay, even though it was only just over thirty miles away.

The door was answered by Sofia's housekeeper. "Come this way." She smiled at us, not asking who we were as Izzy would be recognisable and she was obviously expecting us.

We walked through a hall, which was decorated with many works of art, most of which had a dark theme. Some were rather risqué. Constance poked her head out as Izzy pointed to Martha's Monday Menstruation, which I had to admit, fit Sofia's taste in art well.

We reached her conservatory, which was traditional and looked like a large white bird cage with glass between the bars.

"This is beautiful," I said. "And I'm pleased to meet you." Whilst I had seen her at Branden Bay Halloween Ball and the exhibition, I had not spoken to her.

She looked me up and down. I was in fact wearing designer, just the vintage kind – one of Grandma's dresses to be exact. "How's Connor?" she asked in a strong European accent, which I presumed was Spanish, considering her name, but it did sound more French. She motioned for us to sit down at an iron table with matching chairs.

"He's on the mend, but it'll probably be a while until he receives visitors," I said.

"I've been staying on and off at Millar's hotel, hoping that I can see him. I feel awful. The last time we spoke, I said something bad. But we have always had a fiery..." She paused and then looked at me. "... passionate love." She moved a dark hair from her forehead. "No doubt you've been allowed in?"

"We're not an item," I said in case she wondered.

"Becky's just trying to find out who shot Connor – and her."

"You are here to interview me?"

Well, yes I was, but I didn't want to be that forward. "We're organising a charity event up at Branden Bay Castle to raise money for Connor's favourite cause."

"No doubt that involves cats?"

I nodded.

"One reason that myself and Connor could never be together, is that I'm allergic to them." She sneezed in confirmation.

Constance growled from my bag. "Oh," I said as I pushed her head down. I wasn't sure whether or not Sofia realised Constance was in my tote. I pushed the bag underneath my chair as the housekeeper poured the tea.

"Do you want me to buy a high price ticket?" Sofia asked.

"We were wondering whether you would like to do a fashion show?" Izzy said.

Her eyes lit up. "I am interested. I have a new line and just received a cancellation in Dusseldorf. It would be a superb opportunity to replace it with a local show. When is it?"

"A week Friday."

"So soon? I'm not sure I can get enough local models. Especially for a charity event where they will not be paid."

"Izzy can step in," I said.

"Darling, no. I'm retired." She narrowed her eyes at me.

"No disrespect to Isabella, but I'm using natural women as my models. I ran a market research exercise last year and it told me that women could not imagine themselves in my brand when they looked at models like Izzy. The so say, perfect woman."

Izzy smirked and took a sip of her tea with her little finger sticking out. "I'm glad I got out when I did, darling."

"So, that helps with the recruitment of the models then," I said.

"You, will be the ideal model with your plain looks and curves."

My mouth dropped. The cheek of it. Yes, I'd filled out quite a bit, but plain? I turned to Izzy and she gave a slow shake of her head with her eyes wide open, clearly not wanting me to make a scene. I turned back to Sofia. "I don't really have any relevant experience," I said, feeling somewhat hot under the collar.

"Sweetie, you're a dancer." Izzy smiled. "And personally I think Becky is beautiful and so do a lot of people."

Including Conner, I thought, but did not say. I didn't want Sofia to know she had got to me, even though I could feel the heat coming off my face.

Sofia gestured at me. "Stand up and walk around the room – naturally."

Izzy nodded at me.

I stood up and smoothed down my dress, then walked around the room."

"You will do." She lifted her arm as if performing flamenco.

"I think I'll be too busy on the night with the project management of the show," I said.

"It will only last half an hour and you will be on for five minutes," Sofia said. "I like to have someone famous at each show and whilst no-one knows you outside of the little town you live in, I found that everyone there seems to know who you are."

"Ok, then," I said. At least I would be able to keep a close eye on Sofia.

Izzy raised her eyebrows as if she was super-surprised that I'd agreed to be a model.

Sofia appeared pleased and I was happy that I'd buttered her up and decided to interview her.

"So how long have you known Connor?"

"I met him at one of my shows in Milan. We had a wild weekend." She paused and gave me a small smile.

"He found out I lived in Bath and wanted to promote me and my brand, so invited me to his casino in Bristol to show my designs. It had become an annual event and every now and again, when we're at a loose end we meet up, for ... a while."

I got the picture. "I see. Have you any idea as to who would want him dead?"

Sofia laughed. "He's a bad boy. That's what I like about him. No strings, I'm not ready to settle down and if I was, I would not see Connor as my ideal match. He's obsessed with cats." She laughed. "That is why his sad and desperate wife was dressed up as one at the ball. She's pathetic." She near spat the words out and I noticed her accent now had a cockney edge to it. I wondered whether she had spent a lot of time in London, since moving over from Spain.

What I wanted to ask Sofia, was what she had been doing when Larry had been pushed off the turret at Branden Bay. I knew she was at Millar's that evening, as Helen had told me so.

"So, who else is going to be at the charity event?" she asked.

"Martha Pine," Izzy said.

"Oh, yes, Martha. Did you see her piece on your way in? She has such a unique talent."

I nodded in agreement.

"I like to help fellow artists out," she said. "And we go way back. We trained together."

I guessed if they trained with each other, presumably at art school, she must have known her for some years.

She turned to Izzy. "I saw her at the ball with you. She looked so happy. I'm glad she has found you, Isabella. After the tragedy."

"Yes," Izzy said as she clinked her cup on the saucer and nearly spilt her tea.

I frowned at her. "What tragedy?" I asked. Clearly Izzy had kept something from me.

I felt Constance wriggling in my bag behind my feet.

"Her friend died," Izzy said in a brusque voice, much different from her usual drawl. "Martha will be painting a new piece especially for the event." Izzy seemed to be trying to change the subject.

Sofia was having none of it. "It is so dangerous walking alongside the harbour at night."

"She fell in?" I asked looking at Izzy then to Sofia.

"Yes, drowned. Una was a croupier at Connor's casino," Sofia said, "Didn't Izzy tell you?"

Izzy sipped her tea in silence.

"So sad," Sofia said. "A few people blamed Connor, but that's ridiculous. He's a bad boy but not bad enough to kill a pretty young woman."

Constance dived out of the bag and approached Sofia.

"Where did that come from?" she asked then had a sneezing fit. I guessed a long-haired cat was the worst kind.

Constance had put an abrupt end to our visit and my interrogation.

Back inside the limousine I strapped myself in. I waited until the car was moving so I could not be overheard.

"Why didn't you tell me about Martha's friend working at the casino and drowning?" I hissed at Izzy.

"Isn't it obvious? You would have jumped to conclusions and think poor Martha shot Connor. Which is absurd – of course she wouldn't. She's the most compassionate woman I've ever met. Complicated and moody, yes, but no killer."

"But this is relevant information. She has a motive and she was wearing black," I said. "She was scowling at Connor and you've been giving me the brush off."

"Becky. She didn't do it. And she's not jealous of him, or you."

We travelled home in silence. Was Sofia putting the spotlight on Martha to take the heat off herself? I did not want to alienate Izzy with more questions, she was one of my closest friends. And we had the planned meal at her place with Martha. I didn't want her to cancel it, I needed to check the woman out for myself.

CHAPTER 21

I waited at the café entrance watching the clouds roll in as the waves smashed on the shore. I'd had a few people in the café that day, following a coach trip of pensioners on an early turkey and tinsel trip. It was lovely having the placed filled and buzzing again and it had put a smile on my face and warmed my heart.

I was looking forward to seeing H. I hadn't seen him since our last date, which had ended on a sour note, with him accusing me of being in love with Connor, so I wanted to prove that I only had eyes for him.

He drew up and I went down the path, with Constance in tow.

He got out of the car and we embraced.

"I missed you," he said.

"And you." I squeezed him. "Maybe after the meal

at Izzy's we can come back here? I want us to spend some time together, just us two."

"Sure, come on." He opened the car door for me and I got in.

On the way, we stopped to pick Annie up.

"I'm a bit nervous about meeting Martha," Annie said.

"Why?" I asked.

"I know nothing about art."

"Me neither, but I'm sure there are lots of other things we can chat about." *Like murder,* I thought.

"As long as the discussion doesn't involve Connor Davies, shootings or death," H said. "I want a night off."

"Of course not," I said. Even though I would be plying Martha for information wherever I could and would be watching her like a hawk.

We went through the electric gates to the swanky apartment block carpark. I carried Constance in my bag and Annie held her cat bed. Izzy's place was pristine, so I always kept Constance off her white leather couch. We took the lift and when we arrived at Izzy's apartment, she opened the front door. Once inside, I stopped in my tracks. I was used to Izzy's apartment being so tidy, gleaming with the type of minimalism that made you think no-one lived there. Set up on the polished oak floors was an easel and Martha was there, dressed in a long black overall, splattered with paint of various colours. The white sofas were draped with

Moroccan style throws and Izzy herself was wearing a tie dye kaftan with a scarf tied around her head.

There was the aroma of food cooking. Izzy always ordered in from Corelli's, but on the stove was a pot of something bubbling away, splattering sauce over her usually pristine glass hob.

"Martha's got a lentil dahl and tofu curry on the go. She's vegan, so she's cooking. I don't normally do vegan."

"You don't normally cook, full stop," H said with a laugh.

Izzy swiped him with her hand, then followed through with a hug. "I've missed you big man. How's your case going?"

"No talk about cases, in Exeter or in Branden Bay. I want a stress-free evening."

"Excellent," Izzy said with a small smile in my direction.

I noticed that Martha was continuing to paint and had not acknowledged us, at all.

"We can't interrupt her when she's in the zone, Izzy said. "Let's stay out of her way. She usually paints for about twenty frantic minutes, then breaks off. She has another five to go."

I watched Martha as she dipped her brush into the paint and then pushed it towards the canvass with a grunt.

Constance hissed from my bag and I shushed her.

I gently placed my bottle of bubbly on the marble

worktop, deciding to wait until Martha had finished before I popped the cork, in case I interfered with her creative zone.

Constance dropped to the floor, made her way to Izzy's sofa, jumped up and settled down. I needn't have taken her bed.

"There's bubbly in the fridge, darlings. Help yourselves," Izzy said.

After only five minutes, a timer sounded and Martha put her paint brush down.

"Hello. Sorry to appear rude." She walked towards us in bare feet, which I noticed had red and purple paint on them. "I was in the middle of a creative burst." She removed the black overall and placed it over a stool in front of Izzy's kitchen island. I guessed there would be few splatters of paint on Izzy's white furnishings. Martha wore faded jeans and a washed-out t-shirt and looking at the way Izzy beamed at her, I realised that she was not going to be a great judge of her character, she clearly had Martha up on a pedestal. No wonder she wasn't going to entertain the idea that Martha was on my suspect list.

The meal was very delicious and enjoyable. Martha was clearly a master with spices, and we talked about everything and anything, apart from death.

"What are you painting right now?" I asked Martha.

'My piece for the charity night."

"It's called *The Cat's Purr,*" Izzy said.

"That ties in great with the theme," Annie said. "Maybe Constance can sit for you?"

Constance hissed from the sofa, and we all laughed.

"Admittedly, I'm not a cat fan," Martha said. "I was brought up with dogs, on a farm."

"I told Martha, it's great publicity and her costs will be covered," Izzy said.

Martha smiled at Izzy. "I've got to finish it by tomorrow to give it time to dry. I've booked it in with my printer, so I can produce limited edition prints."

I stared at Martha, could she kill? I would usually have asked Izzy to search the newspaper records to find details about the woman drowned in the harbour, but I knew she would refuse, seeing it as wholly unnecessary. But I decided I would ask Wes, as he worked at the casino.

"I didn't know there was a charity do?" H said.

Annie gave me a sideways glance. "Yes, for Save the Cats."

"Sofia Arbello is going to be there," I said. "I understand you trained together and are friends?" I asked Martha.

She gave a short laugh. "I'd say acquaintances. It wasn't for long. She got kicked out. She's someone who has suspicious connections." She took a drink of wine as we watched. "She loves herself way too much and woe betide anyone who gets on the wrong side of her."

"Really?" I said.

"She prides herself on having the best fashion show on the planet," Izzy added quickly as if trying to change the subject.

"More a show than fashion," Martha said haughtily.

I guessed Martha was not that into fashion and her scruffy appearance confirmed that.

I wished I could have asked more, but H was frowning at me. I was picking up that Sofia had a temper on her. And she had felt scorned by Connor, scorned enough to slap him across the face in public. But was she scorned enough to kill?

After a pleasant evening, we said our goodbyes and left. H dropped Annie on our way home.

Once Annie had shut the car door, H turned to me. "I get the feeling, Becky, that this charity event is one of your schemes to further your investigation."

I remained silent as he drove, but Constance gave a succession of low meows as we travelled the short distance.

H pulled up outside. "Come on then, show me what you've got. I'd like to know what you're up to, before your next suspect dies, like the last one."

I opened the door with Constance in my arms and nervously took him to the snug, where I had moved the murder board and lifted the cloth covering the A-frame.

I left him there while I made us coffee at the professional machine.

I carried the hot drinks into the room, as H studied the board with Constance rubbing up against his legs.

"You suspect Izzy's Martha?"

I nodded. "It's tricky as they seem pretty close."

"She must like her if she's let her trash her place like that."

I laughed. "I know what you mean. But Izzy has been keeping something from me. Martha hates Connor because she was friends with one of his employees, who was found in the harbour."

H shook his head. "Which one?"

I gulped, as Constance gave a low meow. Did Connor really arrange for those who crossed him to be drowned? "It's probably to do with the proximity of the casino and nothing to do with the owner. It was a woman."

He nodded. "A woman drowned there about eighteen months ago. Izzy reported on it as well, if I remember rightly."

"Hopefully, Martha isn't the shooter."

"Be careful, you could lose a friend if you accuse her."

He pointed to the picture of the pink witch. "And who is this cartoon character called Willow?"

"I need to update the picture. I've found her social media. She's a stalker that Connor picked up at his dad's funeral in the summer. She was throwing daggers at Sofia the clothes designer when she was dancing with Connor." I pointed to the picture of Sofia. "She has some sort of on-off relationship with Connor and fell out with him because he cancelled her show due to his divorce. He said she makes a lot of money out of them."

"That's interesting. Connor may have used Sofia's show as a cover for his operation, if she earned that much from it."

I hoped I had not just uncovered something H would give to Brad.

"What about his wife?" H pointed to the wedding photograph.

"Brad is on Helen's case, he thinks that she hired Larry Locke to shoot us."

"I found out he was ex-police, and was going to tell you, then he died."

"Brad thinks Larry fell off the turret as he tried to shoot me."

Constance hissed.

H looked thoughtfully at the board.

"Hopefully they're all coming to the charity event. As you heard, Martha will be showcasing her work. Helen is organising the event, Sofia is doing a fashion show. And somehow, I've got to get Willow there."

"Sofia Arbello at a charity event will be interesting!" H said.

"Yes," I flicked my hair. "In fact, she asked me to be a model."

H threw his head back and laughed.

I stood watching him, then put my hands on my

hips. "Oh, that's nice. I know I'm no Izzy. She said she wants real women."

He put his arm around me. "I'm sure she would love you as her model," he said. "And you'd look amazing. I was just laughing as I know it's the last thing you'd want to do."

It sounded to me as if he was trying to dig himself out of a hole. I picked my drink up from the coffee table and took a sip. *The cheek of it,* I thought, just because I was short, no doubt. Well, that was decided – I would definitely be showcasing Sofia's designs on the catwalk.

We were interrupted by a giggle. I turned my head to see Iona and Jeff pass the door, on their way to the kitchen.

H raised his eyebrows. "Jeff's entertaining then?"

"He's pretty loved up," I said then looked at H. "They see each other all the time."

He took the mug from my hand and placed it on the coffee table then brought me in for a hug. "Hey, I wish I was with you all the time." He kissed me.

Jeff came in. "Oh, sorry," he said. "Do you mind if I make Iona a cappuccino using the café machine?"

She followed him in, wearing the superhero dressing gown I'd bought him for his birthday. It looked odd with her gothic look, and I noticed her make-up was very smudged.

She ran a hand through her raven hair and gave me a brazen smile.

I smiled back but narrowed my eyes at the same time and Constance gave a sassy hiss.

She looked at the murder board. "Did you find out any more details from Martha?"

I shook my head. "Not really." I needed to calm down. "And yes, of course you can make a cappuccino."

H laughed after they had left the room. "I take it you're not too keen on Jeff's new girlfriend?"

"Is it that obvious?"

"Completely."

"It's not that I don't like her. It's awkward when they're here together, I feel the odd one out and this is *my* house."

"If it carries on then Jeff needs to find a place of his own. It's not cool to use your house for his alone time with his girlfriend and then to walk around like that. With their I-just-did-it smiles on."

"I'm glad you noticed," I said. "I've been feeling like a real killjoy. He's saving up to buy somewhere. He saved the reward money I shared out. And he makes quite a bit from his business but I don't charge him rent because he helps me out. Although, he's not here as much now. So maybe I should ask him for some money."

"I agree, it's fine to be charitable, but if you've nothing coming in at the moment from the café, he should be making a contribution."

I was just about to mention the money I'd got from Connor, but decided against it.

"I've an early start in the morning," H said. "The current job feels like it's around the clock. If I'm not working, I'm still going over it in my mind. But if I crack the case, I could be on a fast track to promotion."

I followed him to the door, leaving Constance grooming herself in the snug. I was fed up that we had been interrupted by Jeff and Iona, feeling that they had stolen my last moments with him and put a downer on the evening.

H kissed me goodbye and said he would let me know what he could find on Martha's friend who had drowned. Although, I had already planned to interview Wes.

CHAPTER 22

"I don't think I'll bother darling," Izzy said when I invited her to the casino with Annie and me.

"Are you already going out?" I asked, quite pleased she had said no, as the purpose of the trip was to ask Wes about Martha.

"Martha's away this weekend. I'm taking the opportunity to chill, sweetie."

"Has she an exhibition?"

"No, she's off playing games."

"What? Like chess?"

"No, soldiers."

"Like a medieval reenactment?" I asked imagining Martha in armour.

"No, the reserves, the territorial army. I'm proud of her, giving up her time. But I really have been craving some me-time and I've the whole weekend to myself, so I'm staying put."

"Well, if you're sure?" I thought while my mind raced. If Martha was in the territorial army, she probably knew how to handle a gun.

"I'm waiting for my cleaner, who has been a total darling and agreed to come in for me, and then I'll be relaxing in my whirlpool bath."

AFTER GETTING ready and putting on a smart dress, I met Annie at the end of the road having left Constance wailing in the kitchen. We walked to the station and took the train in, since Jeff was seeing Iona – again. We popped to Connor's apartment first, to give his cats some love. This time I had told Helen we would be there.

After spending half an hour with the cats, who seemed to appreciate our attention, we reached the casino and Annie said hi to the bouncer as we went in. She visited regularly, watching Wes at work, and then stayed at his place afterwards. It seemed that everyone was taking their relationship to the next level, whereas I was not. I was stuck in no-man's land with H.

Annie waved at Wes, then turned back to me. "He's going to join us in his break."

We ordered cocktails. I had a Strawberry Daiquiri and Annie had a Passionfruit Martini with a prosecco shot.

"I love the buzz of the casino," Annie said then sipped her drink.

"It's certainly got an atmosphere of excitement." I looked over to where Connor used to sit, it was empty and had a photograph of him on the Blackjack table, like a shrine.

"Wes said everyone is missing Connor."

"Are you talking about me?"

Annie swung around and reached her arm out to Wes.

He squeezed her hand and kissed her on the cheek, then turned to me. "Hi Becky." He pulled out a stool and sat on it, smiling at me with his soft brown eyes. "I hear you want to ask me about poor Una who ended up in the harbour?"

"Yes, what happened?"

"She fell out with Connor. He thought she'd been stealing from him."

"Was she?"

"She could have been, or she was making genuine mistakes. Either way, she wasn't doing a good job. You have to have your wits about you in this game."

"So, she felt she was badly treated?"

"She was upset." Wes ordered a drink then turned back to me. "According to the report at the time, there was a high level of alcohol in her system when they found her in the water, so the coroner decided that she'd been drunk and had fallen in. A few people blamed Connor."

I gulped. With Connor being so charming to me, and his love of cats, it was easy to forget that he was actually a bad man. "And did anyone make a scene about it afterwards?"

"My boss has a ruthless reputation. No-one crosses him. If someone did think it was him, they wouldn't say it to his face."

I pulled out my phone. "Have you ever seen this woman in here?" I showed him a picture of Martha.

He nodded his head. "Yeah. But I haven't seen her for ages. She used to stand at the bar, but not play."

"She's an artist and was friends with Una."

"Ah. So you think she might have shot Connor?"

Annie put an arm on Wes's hand. "She's friends with Izzy, so don't tell anyone. And she's probably totally innocent."

"You've said to Annie that Connor has a lot of female company?" I said.

He nodded. "There's often a different woman every night at his table. A few regulars. But rarely any trouble. Well, except one girl he likes to avoid. She got drunk here a few weeks ago and caused a scene. Getting upset, babbling on about sleeping with Connor in a coffin, or something. She's off the scale crazy. She screamed that she loved him as security dragged her out. She's not been here again."

"Was her name Willow?"

"Yeah, that's it. We called her Weeping Willow."

Willow, definitely seemed the jealous type.

Although, she was wearing pink at the ball, I needed to check her out, invite her to the charity event and get a feel for her. But listening to Wes, I decided not to go alone.

"And have you picked up on anything concerning Sofia Arbello?" I asked.

He raised his eyebrows. "She's one fiery woman. I've never seen anyone dominate Connor, but she had a good try. It's part of her image, I guess."

"I heard she was upset because he cancelled her show," I said.

"It was a big money spinner, really popular."

I looked back down at my phone. Could any of these women really have shot us, pushed Larry off the turret, torched Larry's shed and tried to run me over? And which of these women could handle a gun? Martha was definitely in the frame. Sofia sounded like she had the sorts of connections where she could pick one up, seeing as her father was part of the underworld. And Willow, she sounded unhinged. Once the weekend was through, I'd been contacting her.

On Monday, Jeff and I left the house for the funeral home. Luckily Iona was working, so I didn't have to think of an excuse as to why I did not want her there. As well as needing someone with me to go and visit Willow, I wanted to spend time with Jeff to build bridges. I'd noticed a lot of tension between us, probably because I was finding it more and more difficult to disguise the fact that I didn't like his girlfriend. Just admitting that fact to myself made me feel much better and as H had said, I shouldn't let them have the run of the place. But still, I wanted to make things right again with Jeff.

"We'll go and visit Willow and then have dinner at Corelli's," I said. "Elena said she is fine with me taking Constance in, as long as we sit at the back." I'd not been to my favourite restaurant for weeks.

We drew up at the funeral parlour, which was just outside Branden Bay on the Bristol Road. It was a double fronted shop, painted dark green with net curtains. We decided to leave a grumbling Constance in the van, and I shuddered as I went in.

A blonde woman at the reception desk looked up. "Can I help?"

"Is Willow available?" I asked.

"She's in, but she's preparing for a funeral. I'll see if she has a few moments. And you are?"

"Becky James."

The woman seemed to recognise my name. "Oh yes, of course." She smiled at me and then left the room.

Willow soon came out. She put her hands on her hips, flicking her long blonde hair. She looked different without the pink wig on. I'd never have recognised her. "You're not here to give me grief, are you?

You wouldn't be the first of Connor's women to give me a hard time."

"I'm not in a relationship with Connor." This was getting a bit tiresome, and Izzy was to blame with her front-page article. "Connor and I work together in a charity business – that's all."

Her expression changed and she smiled. "So, how is he? I'm not allowed to visit him."

"He's still receiving care in the I.C.U."

She lowered her voice. "If he does die, can I preside over his funeral?" Her eyes gleamed bright.

I felt uneasy. "They expect he will make a full recovery."

"Oh," she said. "Can I see him now?"

"He's still not receiving visitors." I wanted to get straight to the point. And I was getting a massive dose of static. Which was no surprise considering the location. "We're holding a charity event this coming Friday at Branden Bay Castle. We wondered whether you'd be interested in coming along as you're a close friend of Connor?"

She appeared really eager. "Wow. Will Connor be there?"

"I'm not sure yet, it depends on what his doctor says. But hopefully, yes." I smiled, knowing Connor would no way be there, but a little lie was surely permitted when investigating a murder. "And he also wondered if you wanted to be involved with planning the event? We're having a meeting at Millar's at five o'clock on Thursday."

"Oh, yes," she said. "I can't wait." She looked at the ornate clock in the reception. "I have to get dressed now, I'm due out in five minutes."

Back in the van Jeff was about to start the engine when his phone rang. "I'll just take this." He picked up his mobile. "Hi, baby."

Urgh, I thought. It just didn't seem right that I was overhearing this conversation.

"Yes, she's here ... the funeral directors. Of course, I do." He paused then lowered his voice. "I love you." He ended the call as his face flushed red.

I looked out of the passenger window as the funeral procession left the undertakers. The body was already on board encased in an oak casket with a pink flower arrangement on top that said 'Nan'. In front of the hearse was a woman, dressed in a black tail suit and a top hat, with a huge black feather stuck in it. She carried a large black cane.

Static ran up my neck.

Constance hissed and pawed at the window.

As the woman passed she caught my eye and smiled.

"It's Willow," I said to Jeff.

"What, the woman in black?" Jeff said and the words hung in the air as we watched the procession pass.

"Let's get home," I said. Dinner in Corelli's would have to wait. I'd lost my appetite.

CHAPTER 23

It was two days before the charity event and I closed the café early. We'd had a couple of nice sunny days so I was busy for a change, but the weather reports warned that a storm was heading our way. I'd cleared my mind of the Halloween shooting. Everything was getting on top of me, it was probably due to months of non-stop action and murders, it was clearly taking its toll. Even though September and October had been free of any mysteries, I'd spent some of those weeks attending court cases, which had brought it all back. I needed a break, so I could look at the current mystery with fresh eyes, and calm down a bit, instead of snapping Jeff's head off every five minutes.

Helen had arranged with Millar's for us to have a meeting room at the hotel to go over the final details of the day together. Sofia and Helen were both booked into rooms there. No doubt Helen had swung that one, as it was for charity. And Millar's were not as busy, as it was nearing the end of November and with the weather being so dark the views from their popular bar and restaurant, were a little grey.

I walked up the road to Millar's, arm in arm with Annie. Constance was allowed to the event itself, as she was the new face of Connor's Charity shop but Sofia had refused to sit in the meeting room with my cat. So she had to stay back at the café with Dannie, who was studying from home.

"I'm impressed with this charity event you're putting on, it's huge," Annie said.

"Helen has done most of the organising. And she will be chairing the meeting."

"But it was your idea," she said.

As we rounded the bend, we saw Izzy stepping out of a limo.

"It's only a five-minute drive," I said. "That must cost her a fortune."

"It's all about the image, I think she pays them monthly and they're not very busy with weddings at this time of year."

We quickened our step as we trudged up the hill and entered the grand reception of Millar's with its black and white tiled floor and pictures of flapper girls on the walls. It had been built in the heyday of the town in the 1920's.

I approached the reception desk. "We're here for the Cat Lovers Charity Ball meeting," I said.

I heard rushed footsteps behind us and turned to see Jeff looking flustered. "I thought I was going to be late. Iona wanted to be involved."

"Maybe Iona is getting a little too clingy?" Annie said.

Iona stepped from behind him.

Jeff blushed and made no comment.

Annie laughed – her usual reaction to embarrassment.

Iona flicked her jet hair. "Jeff asked me to help him with security at the event. My boss was happy to let me have a few days off, as it's for charity. And she's asked head office if they can make a donation."

"The meeting is being held in the Heathcote Room," the receptionist said, gesturing to the corridor.

I gave Jeff my just-wait-til-I-get-you-home stare, then followed the signs to the room and heard the hubbub of voices as we reached it.

"And here she is," Helen said. "Come on Becky, we may as well start."

The four of us found empty seats. Annie and I were together, and Jeff and Iona were opposite us, next to Willow. My heart thumped as I watched them sit down. I was getting really wound up by Iona and had to get my feelings in check, as I needed my wits about me to crack this case.

Helen kicked the meeting off and the main players gave updates on where they were at.

"I've a great selection of models. A real range of all shapes and sizes. I have ten, including Becky who has agreed to join us."

There were some looks of surprise from those around the table and Iona frowned.

"Each of the models will have two to three minutes each on stage with the matador," Sofia said. "The show will last around twenty-five minutes, or so. The finale model will be Becky here, who will be wearing my latest creation - Blushing Bride."

I gave a nervous laugh. I'd been to fashion shows before where the last model stepped out in a wedding dress. I wasn't that keen on that much attention. I certainly didn't expect to be the finale.

Everyone clapped. "Well done for stepping up," Helen said. "The show is always much more popular when the models are celebrities."

"Celebrity?" I said with a laugh. "I wouldn't go that far."

"Everyone knows you around here," Annie said. "You're so brave."

I blushed, I was hoping it was going to be a quick up and down of the runway but two to three minutes with a matador, in a wedding dress, with everyone gawping at me? I pushed it out of my mind and hoped the costume I was going to have to prance around in was not an uncomfortable one. I still hadn't checked out Sofia's collection on-line.

"I need the number of a local florist for the bouquet," Sofia said.

"I have one," Willow said with a smile. "We use them all the time. I can get a discount.' Willow stood up and went to Sofia to give her the number.

"And I'm pleased to report that Millar's have agreed to provide all models, complimentary access to their spa and full use of their technicians," Helen said. "Thanks, Josephine," she gestured to the manager of the hotel who was sitting near us, as everyone clapped in appreciation.

I sat back in my seat and relaxed. Now that was a result — a whole day of pampering. I hadn't been to a spa since the summer and my hair hadn't been cut since I'd moved to Branden Bay. I looked across the table to Iona who was scanning the room, clutching onto Jeff's arm.

"I'll be donating fifty percent of the profits to the charity," Sofia added as Willow returned to her seat.

Everyone clapped.

It was Martha's turn to update, she handed around postcard sized prints.

"I've donated a new piece. I have made fifty limited edition full-sized prints which will sell at fifty pounds each and then the original will be auctioned off after the fashion show.

I looked at the picture of *Feline Purr.* There wasn't even a hint of a cat.

There were oohs and ahhs from those present. Izzy looked on adoringly.

I sighed. I just didn't get it.

"And Becky will be providing some of her bakes," Helen said.

"Cookies," I added. "In the shape of cats. They will be made fresh on the day." I had lined Dannie and Lynn up to help. "I've everything in place, including the cutters." It was going to be a long day.

"And we'll be running the bar with inflated prices to add to the charity pot," Josephine said.

"I've enlisted the help of Andrew Farr who is a well-known local businessman, to run the auction," Helen said. "Thanks to Annie here."

"He's looking forward to it," Annie said.

Helen went through a list of items she had been given for the auction. Including donations from local establishments of free meals and a V.I.P. night at Connor's casino. Willow's employer had also made a very generous donation. Helen peered at Willow. Clearly not happy that her husband's stalker was there, but I'd explained that I needed Willow present, as she was on my list of suspects.

"We're also raffling off a free funeral plan," Willow added with a smile that sent shivers up my spine.

"All bags will be thoroughly searched by Jeff,

before anyone is allowed entry," I said pointing to him with a smile.

Jeff blushed. "Iona is going to help."

"Is this a joke?" Sofia said. "I need proper security at my events to protect my models."

Jeff blushed hard and Iona frowned, looking like Wednesday from The Adam's family as she stared across the room.

"I'll bring my own security," Sofia said. "I have contacts. Especially as the last time we were at the castle someone was shot. I'll ask them to place someone on the door as back up for your ... " She paused and turned her nose up at Jeff and Iona. "Bag checkers."

"I could ask the police to have a presence," Helen said. "But I doubt they'll have the resources."

Sofia put her hand in a stop sign. "No police. Leave it with me."

Helen crossed items off her list as if checking she had covered everything. "So, set up is from two p.m. and we're opening the doors at seven. And I'm pleased to report that Connor is in great spirits and sends his regards and thanks everyone for your help."

Martha pursed her lips.

Izzy put a hand on her arm.

"Thanks for your help, Helen," I said. "It's going to be a great event and hopefully we'll raise a lot for charity."

Josephine stood up. "I'll let catering know that we're ready for the refreshments."

As Helen brought the meeting to a close with a few final words of encouragement, I looked around the room. The whole purpose of the event was to flush out the killer. My neck filled with static, I realised, that it was possible the killer was in the room. Indeed, I hoped they were because if not, I had wasted a lot of time and effort.

I glanced at Helen. As Connor's soon-to-be ex-wife, I would always have to consider her a contender. She admitted she was openly jealous of the women who had slept with her husband and had a lot to gain financially from his demise. She had worn black to the Halloween Ball. Her husband was a known gangster so she must come into contact with criminals with guns. Had she convinced one of them to lend her his weapon? And covered it all up with an elaborate story, setting up solid alibis? She easily fitted the profile of the jealous woman in black that Lady Astrid had given.

Then there was Martha Pine, a woman who hated Connor, that was plain to see, and blamed him for the death of a close friend. She was a woman who not only wore black to the Halloween Ball, I'd noticed that she also wore a black overall when she painted. And she was a member of the territorial army – no doubt she knew how to handle a gun.

Then there was Sofia, one of Connor's closest

women, who also had worn black at the ball. She had been scorned by Connor dropping her shows and I'd witnessed her slap his face. Was she here not because she wanted to help Connor, but to disguise the truth that hell hath no fury like a woman scorned? She was also linked to crime lords across the country and possibly abroad. But was she jealous? If she was, she hid it well.

And there was Willow Wilson, who chatted away to Iona. They looked like opposites, one blonde, one raven haired. There was something dark about Willow. She seemed obsessed with Connor and with death. A woman so intensely jealous she didn't even try to hide it and while she wore pink to the ball, she was a woman who wore black daily for her job. And, as Iona pointed out, she was named after a tree, a woman of the wood.

My phone buzzed on the table as a trolly was brought in with a selection of sandwiches. It was H calling. I answered it.

"Where are you?" he asked.

I walked out of the room with my phone to my ear so I could hear him properly. "At Millar's for a meeting about the charity event."

"They've traced the gun. It's a common weapon. Popular within security and military organisations around the world."

"So, anyone could have used it?"

"It's versatile. An old gun, often used in training with rubber bullets."

I swallowed hard. "Martha has a history in the T.A."

"We're aware of that, Becky. But it's highly unlikely. They think it's organised crime and they've traced the owner. Handguns were banned in the nineties, but it seems this old one was not handed in and is owned by a man. The force local to his address have interviewed him. The gun went missing the same time as his son, who's already done time. They've tightened security up at the hospital."

"What's his name?"

I heard H sigh down the phone. "I can't give you the details, but the prime suspect for the shooting, is definitely a man who has a criminal record and is likely to have joined a crime ring. He's already done time and will have contacts. You need to be careful, and I'm worried about your safety, don't go to that charity event. If he's watching you, he'll know you're going there, it's plastered all over social media."

I shook my head, I knew H was wrong. It was a woman connected to the woods, who wore black, who was jealous. And I would not find out who was trying to kill me, if I didn't attend the charity event. "Have they got Larry's phone? It will possibly have evidence on it, showing the car used to try and mow me down."

"No. They didn't recover a phone." He paused.

"Becky, I mean it. You need to go home and stay home."

"Sorry, I've made a commitment, I'm going."

"Why will you never listen?" H growled down the phone.

After he ended the call, I turned to the sound of my name.

"Becky," Lynn rushed into the reception area. "Sorry I'm late."

"That's okay. The meeting's over, I can update you."

"I managed to get a map of the castle," she said in a low voice lifting a linen tote bag.

"Genius, where from?"

"The library archives. I have a friend from my cards group who works there."

"She's an historian?"

"No, the cleaner. And she needs them back so she can return it to the archives before the end of her shift. We need to take it home now and look at."

"I'll meet you back at mine in half an hour."

I hurried to the meeting room, ate a couple of sandwiches, then called Jeff to one side as Iona chatted away to Willow.

"Iona seems to have made a new friend?" I said.

"Willow says she can get us into the funeral home for a ghost hunt."

I pulled a face. "That's so wrong."

"I think Iona is just helping with the investigation,

Boss. She's just trying to get Willow on-side before she asks her some questions."

"If you say so." I lowered my voice. "You need to come home now, without Iona. I need your help."

He looked nervously behind him. "I brought her up here, though. So I need to drop her back."

"Do what you have to – just come home alone."

BACK AT MY HOUSE, Lynn and I spread the drawings out on the coffee table in the snug and we were soon joined by a flustered looking Jeff.

"Here," Lynn said. "This is the tunnel." She ran her finger over the map.

I kept Constance off the table. I didn't want her to damage these historic items, which we really should not have had possession of.

"And yes, it comes out in the woods, here," she said pointing to the exact place on the map.

I took a collection of pictures with my phone. "Brilliant."

"I'll get this back to Dora."

"You're amazing, Lynn. We need to get up to the castle," I said. "And I really want to speak to the spirit of Lady Astrid."

"But I'm banned," Jeff said.

"We'll stand outside then. At the foot of the turret. I have to make contact."

"What are you going to ask?"

“I’m going to ask who shot me and who pushed Larry off the top?”

“It’s already getting dark,” Lynn said. “We don’t want to be spotted.”

“We’ll park the van down the hill and walk the last half mile,” Jeff said.

CHAPTER 24

Walking up to the castle was a very blustery and wet experience. The expected storm had well and truly arrived. I pulled my coat to my body, clutching onto my tote bag with Constance inside. I marched ahead, determined to discover who the killer was. Gone was my usual fear. We didn't speak as we walked up there as the sea breeze was loud in our ears. As we turned the corner, I heard a car pass.

I looked up but it had already passed. "Did you see who that was?" I called to Jeff.

He lifted his head as the rain beat against us and shook his head. We carried on up.

"Maybe this wasn't such a good idea," Lynn shouted as she held onto a lamp post. "That's some wind."

We reached the outside of the castle. I touched the

walls as the wind blew me, trying to get a connection but I could feel nothing, other than the weather. There was no way I could relax enough to connect.

"We could go inside," Jeff shouted.

"How? You've been banned."

He lifted his set of keys. "I've still got these."

Lynn took them. "I need to get inside, I'm wet through."

I nodded, I wanted to get out of the cold as well and was prepared to deal with the consequences, the weather was wild.

Once inside the three of us pushed the door closed and Jeff turned his flashlight on. It was quiet except for the high-pitched whistle of the wind getting between spaces around the windows. I let a bedraggled Constance out of my bag. She was wet and I smiled, it reminded me of the first time I'd let her in my house, she'd been wet through and had looked so bedraggled.

Constance gave a loud and grumpy meow.

"Let's nip up to the turret, before someone comes," I said. "It may have been a security guard that passed us on the road, and they might be back soon."

Static filled my body as we ran along the corridor, presumably from the various spirits. But when we reached the turret, it was quiet. Eerily quiet.

I looked at Lynn and frowned. "Can you feel anything?"

She shook her head. "No."

I felt a chill as I climbed the stone steps. "Nothing." I shook my head. "She's not here."

Jeff held up his EMF meter. "I'm not picking anything up, at all."

"Well that's odd isn't it?" I said.

"Maybe she moved on, lovey," Lynn said. "Tired of our world with the shootings and killings. The other side must seem more appealing now."

"But how am I going to discover who shot Connor and killed Larry?" I said.

"With your regular detecting skills, lovey."

"While we're here, shall we look for the tunnel?" Jeff asked.

I nodded, pulling up the pictures I'd taken of the map with my phone. "We need to go to the far end of the main floor, there are some steps down. But let's be quick in case security comes back."

We hurried through and I felt buzzing, as before. We reached a door and I tried it, but it was locked. I felt static in my hand and Constance gave a huge hiss and her coat bushed out as much as was possible while it was wet.

"From the map, it looks as if this door leads to a corridor that splits into two and the left side will lead to the tunnel," I said.

"But it's locked," Jeff said,

"The shooter must have a key, as this must be how they got in and out. I'll let H know and he can feed the information through, maybe get a key from the castle administrators." I shivered. "The last thing we need is to be arrested for trespassing, so let's get back. I'm soaked through and I don't want us getting a chill — we have to be fit for the charity event."

"I'm sure we'll flush the killer out," Jeff said.

I sighed. "We have to."

I'D BEEN REALLY pleased when Sofia had booked me into Millar's for a make-over. I was so in need of a trim. But I sulked as I sat in the hairdresser's chair having spent half an hour in a treatment room, being waxed. The hairdresser popped off to check another model who had foils in her hair.

I caught Izzy's gaze reflected in the mirror and crossed my arms. "I'm still stinging."

"It's an essential part of modelling, sweetie." Izzy laughed. "Us models always have to de-fuzz before a show."

"It was a bit extreme," I said. "The woman even waxed my toes as if I was a hobbit." Some of the waxing had seemed entirely unnecessary.

"You're the one that agreed to do it," Izzy said. "Skip the blow dry and let's sit in the spa after this. I'm in need of some warming up, then I'll treat you to lunch before you get your nails done."

Having had a steam, and a sauna I'd forgotten all

about the waxing as the aromatherapy eased my mood and relaxed my body.

We ate lunch wearing soft white dressing gowns.

"The charity event is a lot of effort to go to, darling. Do you think you'll be able to unmask the killer?"

"I hope so."

"My money is on Sofia. Considering she's from the London Underworld. And there's the solider training she did with Martha. She must have been kicked out for a reason."

"Wait. Sofia trained in the Territorial Army? I thought she went to Art School with Martha."

"Whatever gave you that idea?"

"I just assumed."

Izzy shook her head. "Maybe you're losing your touch, sweetie."

I was pleased that Izzy was finally taking an interest in the case, but was none too pleased at her criticism. "But Sofia is Spanish. What's she doing in the army reserves?"

Izzy laughed. "Sweetie, Sofia is her business name. Her real name is Sandra Ash. There's nothing Spanish about the woman. It's put on for her image. And it works, clearly, if you fell for her phoney accent."

"Why does she use a Spanish name?"

"Because of the Bull Fighter theme, you know, at her shows."

"Bull fighter? I've never seen any of her shows."

Izzy stared at me for a long moment. "Oh ... sweetie."

I tutted. "I'm sorry to be so ignorant of the artistic world." *Really*, I thought. I felt so judged about my lack of appreciation of art and now I was being mocked because I didn't follow the latest fashion trends. "My background is in acting, singing and dance. But I'll find out soon enough tomorrow."

"Indeed, you will," Izzy said, looking slightly worried as if I wasn't going to be able to be a good model. I mean, all I had to do was walk up and down the catwalk. Izzy peered at me over her green drink. "You have researched Sofia's designs at least?"

"Of course, I have," I snapped, while telling myself to google her when I got home.

But when I finally reached my house, I was so tired, I fell asleep. I needed an early night as I had a big day ahead of me.

CHAPTER 25

I had left it late to arrive at the charity event as H's regular texts warning me to be careful had made me nervous. Constance poked her head out of my tote bag as I entered Branden Bay Castle, passing the security which Sofia had laid on. They were extremely burley looking guys. Jeff and Iona had been relieved of bag-checking duties as Sofia's security contact was dealing with everything.

As I entered the main room, there were many people rushing around, setting out chairs, putting up posters and decorations. There was only one hour to go until opening time. The buzz of excitement was amazing. I had to hand it to Jeff and Iona, they were working hard as they set up the P.A. system. Iona spoke into the microphone and smiled at Jeff who gave her the thumbs up that she was coming out loud and clear. Dannie and Lynn were setting out the cat shaped cookies and leaflets promoting the cafe with money off vouchers.

I took a deep breath, everything was in order.

"Becky, there you are," Izzy said. "Sofia wants to get everyone together and in their underwear."

Oh? She provides underwear? I thought, but did not say it out loud, obviously another thing I didn't realise about being a model.

"I need to pass Constance to Jeff, I can't get her near Sofia otherwise she'll start sneezing."

After I'd handed Constance over, Izzy took me by the arm. "Come along, Sofia's waiting and we need to keep a close eye on the woman." Izzy had gone from not taking much interest in the case to pushing me along with it.

We went to a room which led off the main event space. Inside were various women wearing underwear, presumably waiting for the fashion outfits to arrive. I averted my gaze. I'm not a communal changing room type of person.

"Ah, our famous model," Sofia said putting on a Spanish voice. Now I knew she was faking it, her accent did sound a little over the top. "Zelda, hair and make-up on Becky James please."

Izzy took me over to a mirror with a chair in front of it. "Sit, they only have an hour to get you looking ready for the runway."

I gave a few yelps as Zelda teased and twisted my hair. She sleeked it back into a Spanish style and slapped on a huge splat of gel, then braided the rest of my hair down my back. She made my eyes up, with even more kohl than Iona used, and stuck on huge eyelashes, which looked like two black moths had landed on my face. She drew me a couple of fierce and dark eyebrows. As I looked in the mirror, I jumped. I hardly recognised myself.

I looked around but still could not see the rail of dresses – Sofia was really leaving it to the last moment.

"Stand up and I'll help you into it," Izzy said with a worried look on her face as she held a huge white feather in her hand with some material attached to it.

"What's that?" I asked. "Some sort of head dress?"

She lifted it up against her body and I saw with horror it was a skimpy bodice with a white feather train attached to it.

She bit her lip. "I take it you lied when you said you had looked Sofia up?"

"I can't wear that!" I hissed.

"What seems to be the problem?" Sofia called from across the room.

My bottom lip quivered.

"You can't back out now, darling," Izzy whispered. "Sofia only agreed to it because she had a local celebrity as a model."

"But, Izzy."

"She could be the shooter, you said so yourself."

I undressed and allowed Izzy to help me into the creation. I looked in the mirror at the tight white lace body, which had strategic modesty pads in it, thank goodness.

"It's the least revealing of the entire collection. It could be worse," she said as a model passed us in a black creation, which left little to the imagination and I realised why we all had to have the extreme waxing.

"Come on, you lot, line up," Sofia called out in a more aggressive voice. Her Spanish accent seemed to be fading.

What on earth am I doing? I thought.

"Don't worry, sweetie, photography is banned at this event, so you won't be plastered all over social media."

Sofia approached us to check me over. "What are those yellowy brown marks up your legs and on your butt?"

I looked behind, seeing that the outfit was quite cut away. "They're fading bruises."

She pointed at Zelda. "Get rid of it," she shouted in pure Cockney.

I stood as Zelda used a large quantity of designer brand concealer on my body.

My stomach lurched as I heard cheers from the audience as Sofia launched her show. I waited for the longest twenty minutes of my life, while each of the nine models before me went out and strutted their stuff.

"And finally for the matador to feast his eyes on, we

have the famous Becky James," Sofia called in her returned Spanish accent from the stage.

There was riotous applause. I thought I was going to vomit.

I stepped out, my legs shaking feeling the feather train dragging behind me as I walked along the runway. The first person I saw was Jeff, with Constance in his arms. His mouth dropped as if he was staring at his mother singing *Sex Bomb* at the karaoke. Iona sat beside him frowning and then crossed her arms, clearly not approving. I have to say, I didn't approve of myself either. Willow smirked at me in a way that made me shudder. Annie waved and clapped and Wes gave a whistle. Martha looked on, expressionless, just staring. Before me was the matador — he wore a hat and held a red cape.

"Act," Izzy shouted at me from the side-lines.

I pointed at the matador and he stepped back and flapped his cape. I got into my stride, as my performing arts training came flooding back. The crowd certainly loved it and I smiled, thinking it was not so bad, as I put my hands up to my head to mimic horns and scuffed my left foot. Having passed the matador who had dramatically flung himself on the floor, I reached the end of the runway. The smile from my face slipped away as I saw an open-mouthed H.

He stared at me. His face was crimson, his dark eyes, bore right into me.

Oh, no, I thought, *what on earth is he doing here?* I

gave a short smile and about-turned, then sashayed down the runway to where the other models stood. Sofia pulled the Matador up from the floor and danced a few bars of flamenco with him as the audience applauded.

When she stopped she approached me and lifted my arm as if I'd just won a boxing match, then we took a double bow to an even louder applause.

"Becky, you're a natural," Sofia gushed as we returned to the changing area. "And you look amazing. I'm sure I'll be inundated with orders. And please keep the body, it's yours, she said as she unclipped the feather train." Meet me later. I want to make you an offer. Don't bring Izzy, just yourself."

I gulped. There was no way I was meeting her alone. Did she plan to kill me?

I found my clothes and looked out for Izzy. I needed to change out of my outfit, but she was nowhere to be seen, so I just pulled my dress on, over my body and stuffed my own underwear back into my tote bag.

Once in the main event room Andrew Farr was conducting the auction, holding up Martha's original painting. Izzy was by her side.

Dannie rushed over. "Wow, you looked hot! Did you see the look on H's face?" she said with a giggle.

"He looked well ticked off," I said.

"I'm not sure that's how I'd describe it."

"Has anyone seen anything suspicious," I said.

"No, nothing."

"Becky," I heard the gruff voice behind me. It was H.

I shut my eyes and took in a deep breath, before reopening them. I turned around as Dannie inched away.

"Nice of you to come," I said in a high voice.

"You're too exposed," he said.

I put my hands on my hips. "Sorry, if I embarrassed you."

"What? No not that. I want you out of this place. Your safety's at risk. There's been a development."

"I'm not going anywhere, unless you give me enough detail, to convince me I should leave."

"They attended the house of the son who stole the gun and found his property long-term empty. The neighbour had never seen him, as she's a new tenant of the owner. After we checked with the landlord, she told us that he had a hut in the woods." H stopped as a group of models passed us towards the event space.

I took a breath, as static fizzed in the nape of my neck, remembering the dream I'd had, of a hut in woods.

"We found his decomposing body roughly buried nearby."

"So the guy who had the gun, is dead? And was shot in some woods? Where?"

"On the edge of Exmoor."

"So who has the gun now?" I asked.

"He had a girlfriend and after checking with her estranged family, they've not seen her for six months."

"So his girlfriend and the gun are missing? Who is she?"

"Her name is Vicky Richards, she's in her twenties, and has at times displayed psychopath tendencies. She left without medication and has not attended her regular doctor appointments."

"So you think she shot him and took the gun?" I said.

He nodded

I looked over at Sofia who was chatting to Martha. Both of them were at least thirty.

"The last time there was any activity in Vicky's bank account was about five months ago. She's likely to have assumed a new identity. They're sending over a mug shot to Brad but apparently, she's about five foot three and blonde."

Dannie returned to us with a cat shaped cookie in her hand. "Are you okay?" she asked me. "You look like you've seen a ghost."

"We need to get Becky back home, now," H said.

"Where are Jeff and Iona?" I asked Dannie.

"They left ten minutes ago with Willow," she said.

"What about Constance?" I asked.

"They took her with them. They're going back to the house to drop her off, as she was restless. Really restless. I'm sure she's fine, it's too busy in here for her, and loud. Then they're going to the funeral parlour."

"Oh, no." I put a hand to my mouth.

"Hey, Becky, it's fine. They said not to worry, they'll be back to help clear up," Dannie said.

I turned to H. "They're in danger. Willow is blonde, and not much taller than me. When I looked her up on social media the only account I could find was one opened in the summer."

"That's not good," H said.

"I told you it was a woman."

"What's going on?" Dannie asked.

"They've traced the owner of the gun," I said. "They think it ended up in the hands of a blonde woman in her early twenties, who's a psychopath."

Dannie put her hands to her chest. "What, Willow?"

"It could be," H said. "Let's get out of here."

I was petrified as H drove us back down the hill. I could hardly speak and shook as Dannie had her arm around me as we sat on the back seat. We'd called Jeff but he wasn't answering.

"Jeff could be in extreme danger," I said. "And Constance."

"And Iona," Dannie added. "Check the G.P.S." She pointed to my phone.

I pulled up the app with my hands shaking. "It says Constance is in the house." But she wasn't the only one I was nervous about.

We pulled up outside.

"Jeff's van isn't here," I said.

"Maybe he parked at the spiritualist hut?" Dannie said.

A police car drew up behind us.

I opened the door and called out. "Jeff?" But all was quiet.

I called his number again, but it went straight to voicemail. I left another message asking him to call me immediately.

"Constance," I called. Although the G.P.S tracker said she was in the house, I would not be happy until I felt her fluffy body in my arms.

"Connie cat."

Silence.

I looked at the tracker and followed the blue blob which told me where my cat was until I reached the kitchen. I frowned, at the centre of the table was a Victoria sponge. Seeing a small grey piece of plastic sticking out, I lifted the top to find Constance's G.P.S. collar nestled in the butter cream.

CHAPTER 26

"You stay here," H said. "She may no longer have the gun, but that doesn't make her any less dangerous. She's a confirmed psychopath who shot you and tried to run you down.

"If she stuck Constance's collar in the sponge, where's Constance and where are Jeff and Iona?" I choked on my tears.

"Maybe she's locked them in the morgue?" Dannie said.

"Let's all calm down," H said. "At the moment, Willow has no idea that we're on to her. Uniform are on their way over to the funeral home, and Brad's team are in a convoy to Branden Bay as we speak."

"Brad won't update us on what's happening, he hates me. And it's my cat and Jeff's like family."

Dannie put her arm around me and turned to H.

"He's like a brother to me as well. We need to know what's happening."

He ran a hand through his hair. "There's uniform outside, to protect you. I'll go to the funeral parlour so I can find out and put your minds at rest. But don't move."

After he had left, we sat at the kitchen table in silence, too tense to even have a tea.

I took a deep breath. "I don't know about you, but I can't just sit here." I breathed out slowly. "I sense Jeff and Constance are in immense danger."

"Don't, Becky. I can't cope with it," Dannie said with tears in her eyes. "But as H said, Willow doesn't know the police have found her ex-boyfriend's body. And it's not Jeff and Iona she wants dead, or Constance. It's you."

I shuddered. "And for no good reason other than I danced with Connor, the guy she's obsessed with?"

"Yeah, but as H said, she's a psychopath."

I shook my head. "Can you get the laptop? I just want to go over everything."

Dannie left and returned within one minute passing me the laptop and opened up the spreadsheet which she used for collating the clues in. "I'll make us a tea while you're going through it."

I scanned the evidence we had collected over the previous three weeks, one piece at a time, until my blood ran cold.

I stood up. "Oh, no."

Dannie swung around with the milk in her hand.

"Leave that," I said. "We have to go – now."

"STOP A MINUTE," Dannie called as she held her side. We'd snuck out the back way, through the gate, passed the spiritualist hut onto Castle Road then cut through to the residential area. "I've a stitch."

"Work through it, we're nearly there," I called back to her.

As I reached the front door of the building Iona lived in, shocks of static coursed through my hands. I'd only been with Jeff once when he dropped her off but thankfully, I remembered where it was. "They're here, I sense it," I whispered. I lifted the hand I had my phone in and texted H to tell him exactly where we were. I hadn't before, as I knew he would have told us to stay put.

I opened the communal door and took the stairs. Dannie followed me up to the fourth floor.

As we reached the top, I felt I had no breath left until I heard a loud meow.

"No," Jeff shouted.

Dannie and I both barged against the door, which opened. We fell in and both landed on the floor. It wasn't locked. Static raged over my whole body as I looked up.

Iona stood wide eyed. Behind her were shelves full of dolls. I put my hands to my ears, the noise was deafening. A chorus of *help me, release me, let me go,* filled my head. I realised what I was looking at, was a collection of captured spirits.

Jeff was cuffed to the bed. "Iona stop this."

Iona held a red haired Victorian style doll in her left hand and had Constance by the scruff of her neck in the other. "Come to me, spirit. Leave the cat and find a new home." She looked from Constance to the red-haired doll.

I jumped to my feet. "Put her down," I screamed as Dannie held onto me. "She's not possessed."

"In the doll, now!" Iona shook a wailing Constance as she held her by the scruff of her neck. Constance was powerless to defend herself.

"What are you doing?" Dannie shouted at Iona, while still holding me back.

Iona took two spaces and held Constance out of the window, dangling her outside.

Now, cats can land on their feet, but maybe not from the fourth storey.

"Baby, don't," Jeff gasped from the bed. He looked over to me. "I'm sorry."

"Shut it," Iona said to Jeff then laughed as she gazed at me. "I want to hurt you as much as you hurt me."

"What on earth have I done?" I said.

"You couldn't let him go, could you. You couldn't let me have him. He's my boyfriend. Not yours. You treat him like a slave. You've brain washed him. But he's mine."

"Baby, I told you over and over again. Becky's like a sister to me. And please, don't hurt Constance."

"The cat's possessed, you fool. None of you can see it and you're supposed to be paranormal detectives?" she scoffed. "I need to remove the spirit from her and add her safely to a doll, where I can be her guardian. Like the other's I've saved."

I looked to the shelves where the spirits wailed. "Jeff, the dolls are possessed. How have you not picked that up on your E.M.F meter?"

Iona laughed. "As if I was going to let him bring that thing in here."

I glanced back at the shelf. The dolls were surrounded by interspersed colours, like smoke, integrating with each other. The spirits realised I could hear them and started calling my name. Each one desperate to be released. I looked back to Iona as my body stung with static. "You're not their guardian, you're their jailer."

"They love me."

I shook my head. "I can hear their tears, they despise you."

"Don't make her angrier," Dannie whispered in my ear.

Dannie was right, I needed to calm down. Months of putting up with Iona was rising to the top and I felt enraged. But Constance's life was as risk, in fact all our lives were at risk, I had to focus and push my emotions aside.

"I swore to never love again," Iona said lowering her arm with the doll in it. "Why do people always steal my men?" She stared at me. "So, you worked it out did you?"

"You're a woman who wears black, pretty much all the time. You were at the castle when Larry was pushed and it seems that you're jealous of me. It was nothing to do with Connor, he just got in the way."

"As if that crook matters. The world would be a better place without him, but yes, he took the bullet for you."

"It was you that nearly ran me down and Larry traced you."

"I saw him watching you, then spotted him on the prom, taking down my number plate. I doubled back and tailed him all the way back to that allotment of his. But it was busy."

"But why kill Larry?" I asked.

"He begged me not to. He said he'd keep it all to himself, and no-one would ever know." She laughed. "Well after that, he definitely had to die."

I gulped and hoped H would hurry up, she clearly intended to harm us all.

"So, you torched his shed the next morning."

"She couldn't have done that," Jeff said. "I was with her all night and all morning."

"By the state of you when you got home, I'm

guessing she drugged you. That's why you kept sleeping in and missing your shift."

Constance was being uncharacteristically quiet as Iona still clutched her by the scruff of her neck.

"Lady Astrid referred to you as the woman of the woods," I said. "I guess that's because you killed your boyfriend in a wood. Spirits are all seeing."

"What boyfriend?" Jeff asked.

As soon as I said Lady Astrid's name, I heard her calling me from the shelf. I put my hands to my ears, but it did not stop, I could still hear her inside my head.

"I spoke to Astrid, a lot, before I rescued her," Iona said. "She was a good listener." Iona's eye twitched.

I was glad that I was keeping her talking but at the same time, worried I was pushing my luck. "Why kill your boyfriend, an innocent man?"

"He wasn't innocent. He stole the gun from his Dad. He wanted us to hold up post offices. Then I saw him sleeping with the next-door neighbour. I didn't tell him, I knew. I asked him to go over to the woods for some more shooting lessons." She paused. "It was quick. I was going to do the neighbour too, but she was always with her friend and then they went off travelling to Australia."

"I heard your real name is Vicky and you're blonde underneath that dyed hair," I said.

"You think, you're so clever. But no, you're still

stupid. You thought I got into the castle through a blocked-up tunnel."

"That did confuse me yes, but now I presume you drugged Jeff and copied his keys. And mine so you could go into my house and leave Constance's collar there." I turned my gaze to my cat. She was still quiet, but now glowed a purplish pink.

Iona followed my gaze and lifted her arm to check my cat.

I heard Grandma's voice in my head. *The cat is safe. Get her, now.*

I looked around for Grandma's spirit, but couldn't see her. The possessed dolls joined in with a chorus. *Do it now. Do it now.*

Without thinking I charged at Iona. As she fell to the floor, I heard Jeff calling to Dannie, telling her where the key to the handcuffs was. I spread out over Iona, covering her body with my dead weight as she struggled beneath. I sobbed as I stared at her empty left hand. My cat was no longer in it.

I felt Jeff lift me off Iona. As he did, she looked up at him, with adoring eyes, as if he was pulling me off her, for her benefit. Rather than the real reason, which was so that he could restrain her, instead of me. She scrambled to her feet, just as H entered the room.

Jeff pushed me to the side as Iona charged at him. But when she reached him she flung her arms around him, crying. "You saved me. I love you, so much."

H stood in front of me as uniformed police thumped up the stairs.

Constance is fine, Dannie called from the window. "She's landed on a ledge by the fire escape."

Jeff stood with Iona, his face flushed and eyes full of tears. I could tell he had really loved her.

"I had to protect you, to protect our love," Iona said through a sob, as she looked up at him. "I did it for you, Jeff. I wanted you to love me and only me. To be mine."

Jeff nodded at H who proceeded to read Iona her rights, while she was cuffed by uniform.

As soon as she was restrained, I rushed to the window and looked out, to see Dannie climbing down the fire escape with a uniformed officer, having rescued Constance.

I ENDURED an endless interrogation by Bad Cop Brad who wanted to go through the full events since Halloween. Iona had been passed over to the hospital for assessment. And all Brad seemed to want to know was whether I was laundering money for Connor Davies, as they'd found ten thousand pounds in my bank account. I was rescued by Rachel, H's sister. She was a lawyer on maternity leave but had frequently helped me out.

Brad stood up and growled at me. "As soon as I have anything on Davies, whenever that is, I'm getting you back in. Even if it's years from now." He near screamed at me. "I know you're on his payroll."

Rachel rose from her chair and faced him. "D.C.I. Harris, if you ever speak to my client like that again, you will be receiving papers from me concerning police harassment."

He left the room.

"Wow," I said. "He's got issues."

As we left I found Smith waiting in the reception. She was huge. She smiled at me "Becky."

I approached her. "Wow, when is it due?"

She bit her lip. "Them, I'm expecting triplets."

No wonder Brad was stressed. "Sorry, I seem to have upset the father." I nodded behind me.

She sighed. "I think the pressure has got to him. Please accept my apologies if he has been rude to you."

"Good luck," I said. "I'm sure he'll mellow out when they're born."

THE WHOLE of the next day and evening, I spent at Carol's after Rachel had dropped me there. H had popped in with Constance on his way back to Exeter. Carol didn't let me out of her sight.

Dannie had been with her parents and Jeff had stayed at his mum's. He was obviously, really upset about Iona. Although her real name was Vicky, we would always think of her as Iona. And it seemed his real mum had hated her even more than she hated me. As much as he had fallen out with his mother, she was the one he wanted to spend time with. I also missed my parents but knew they would be calling me the following day as it was my birthday. Although, I was keeping that quiet from the rest of the world.

I WOKE up in Carol's spare room, on my birthday, to a video call from my parents. Their tanned and happy faces beamed at me. "Happy birthday to you, Happy birthday to you ..." they sang. Both of my parents had beautiful voices and I smiled as they performed it well — although I stuck my headphones into my mobile as I didn't want anyone in the house to hear them. I intended to keep my birthday a secret, I wanted to spend a quiet week, while I planned my Christmas themed cakes for the café, as it was nearly December. No doubt Izzy would be publishing a whole article about the Halloween Ball and what happened, and that was bound to draw everyone back to the café, it always did.

"Your birthday present is to tell you that we've booked our ferry home. We're going to be with you in three weeks time."

I burst into tears. It had been nearly two years since I'd seen them.

Mum cried too.

Dad coughed. “Come on you two, pull yourselves together.”

THE REST of the day I spent fighting with Carol to get home. First it was stay for brunch, then she wanted me to help redesign her bedroom and choose fabrics and furniture on-line. Then it was afternoon tea and finally, as she had a date-night with Paul, she suggested I went home. I had a shower and then returned to the spare room to find my clothes missing. Dannie had packed me some clothes but all that was left was a dress. I realised Carol must have whacked everything in her washing machine.

I pulled the dress on and dried my hair, glad that I’d had it cut at Millar’s salon. I felt a whole lot better – even normal, if there is such a thing.

“I may as well walk back,” I said as I went downstairs.

“Paul and I will drop you on our way. And you have Constance, it’ll be easier in the car.”

I picked my cat up, went outside and got in their car.

As we drew up, I saw that the curtains were drawn in the café. *That’s odd*, I thought.

Paul and Carol followed me in and Constance jumped to the ground, pawing at the internal door to the café. I opened it to see what was going on.

“Surprise.”

All my friends were there, even Connor Davies in a wheelchair.

And at the front H. "You didn't think we'd forget your birthday, did you?"

I laughed. "I've never told you when my birthday is."

"I've had access to your police records, in the past," H said.

"And I've completed countless forms for you," Dannie said. "Obviously with your date of birth on."

"And I know when it is," Marcus said sheepishly as he came to the front.

I laughed. "What are we waiting for?"

Dannie turned on the music and Izzy handed me a glass of fizz then pointed to a table full of wrapped gifts.

Connor wheeled himself over to me and handed me an envelope.

"How are you doing?" I asked.

"I've been released. It turns out the police had asked the hospital to keep me in for longer than necessary."

"That's a bit cheeky," I said.

"Yes," Connor said. "Especially as I was in a private room and paying for it."

"I'm so pleased you came."

"The policeman invited me, so I had to show up." He nodded over to H. "He's a good man."

I took his hand. "Now it's my turn to apologise. All

this time the world was blaming you for bringing a shooter and killer to Branden Bay and it was nothing to do with you at all. The bullet was meant for me."

"I would gladly take a bullet for you, Becky. There's not too much long term damage, I just need time to heal."

I smiled, Connor had mellowed through his injuries. "So are we still opening the charity shop?"

"Of course, the grand opening is on Monday. After that, I'm off to the Canaries." Connor beckoned Helen over.

"Really?"

"I have a villa over there. The weather is milder, it's better for me to stay there. The cold and winter bugs are not good if you're recovering from a punctured lung. It's going to take a while to get there, as I've been advised not to fly so will be travelling by car and ferry. And I'm going to write a thriller." He pointed across the room to my ex. "Marcus is going to help."

"You're taking him with you?" I said with a smile.

He lowered his voice. "I'll kill two birds with one stone, he can type my words as I dictate, and I can keep him away from my sister."

I laughed. "Poor Marcus."

Connor smiled. "Not poor, he'll be well paid."

Marcus waved as he stood with Tara.

"Looks like a real bromance," I said.

"I like the guy."

"Me too," Helen said now at his side. "He keeps you

on the straight and narrow, Mr Davies." She looked at me. "I'll be overseeing the casino. I've enjoyed it."

Connor took her hand. "We're putting the divorce on hold. She's a decent woman, my wife. We could never have settled on the financial aspect of the divorce, we're both as strong as each other. I realised, while I lay in that hospital bed – we make a great team."

"Good luck," I smiled at them both as Helen squeezed his shoulder.

Izzy and Annie approached me as Helen wheeled Connor towards the buffet table.

"I'm doing a piece this week on the charity shop," Izzy said. "I'll combine it with a report on your latest case."

"I was kind of clueless throughout this one."

"Rubbish," Annie said. "You said straight away it was a jealous woman who wore black and the police ignored you. And you never liked Iona. That's probably why."

I glanced up at Izzy. "Sorry that I thought it might be Martha."

"No worries sweetie," she said, then gave me a hug.

"Where is she?" I asked.

Izzy stepped back and flicked her hair. "She's gone to Scotland. I'm not speaking to her. She exploded at me. Do you know what she said?"

"What?"

"That I'm ... high maintenance." She pouted.

Annie laughed.

"What's so funny? I just wanted the place to be a bit tidier, and I like nice things. I'm the one that paid for everything too. She said I was privileged and entitled."

"Sorry, Izzy," Annie said as she tried to suppress her smile.

"I worked hard for my money."

"We know that," Annie said.

"And she said I was a total flirt." She moved a hair from her forehead.

Constance meowed at her feet and Annie and I did not hold back our laughter.

Izzy picked my cat up. "Thanks for the sympathy, you're such a beautiful and amazing kitty." She kissed her head and walked away with Constance still in her arms.

Annie was accosted by Andrew Farr who wanted a dance.

I went over to Jeff and put my arm in his. "Cheer up."

"I loved her," he slurred, clearly drowning his sorrows at the punch bowl.

"I know, the first broken heart is the worst." Although I had to admit, as break-ups go, Jeff's had trumped any of mine. Finding out your girlfriend is a psychopathic killer ... is not ideal.

"Come and dance with me and Blue," Dannie said to Jeff pulling at his hand. "Have you told Becky?"

"What?" I asked.

"We're taking him to London for a couple of days to cheer him up. Blue got us free tickets to a premier for the latest action hero film in Leicester Square. Her brother lives in London and has a security firm."

Jeff smiled. "It's gonna be insane." He put his drink down and allowed Dannie to drag him away.

Lynn tapped me on the shoulder. "Just to let you know, lovely. We've been releasing the spirits, one by one." Lynn and her circle of mediums had collected the dolls. H had convinced Brad to allow them to be removed from the scene.

"What about Lady Astrid of Cleve?" I asked.

"We put her back at the castle. Some of the spirits were moved on, but some of them like to walk amongst us."

I shivered, didn't I know it. "It's really creepy."

"Not as creepy as Iona. Hopefully she will stay out of circulation. Come and have a dance."

After the track had ended and everyone had sung happy birthday, I blew out twenty-seven candles, while H held the cake.

I wandered over to the glass café doors with Constance in my arms, I held her close not wanting to let her out of my sight. I looked out at the seaside scene. The sun had broken through the clouds and the prom looked pretty and the sand glinted. I felt warm inside that Branden Bay was my home. I glanced down at my hand, in which I had Connor's envelope. Written on it was: *For you and the policeman.* I placed Constance at my feet and opened it. Inside was a voucher for two nights at a luxury hotel in Devon.

I blushed as H came over. That would be a bit more serious than our relationship was. I'd already made it quite clear, that sort of thing was not going to happen long-distance.

"Thanks, for the party." I gestured around the room as H reached me.

"It was a team effort," he said. "Sorry, I haven't had a chance to sort out a present. But I have news." He took me in his arms. "I wrapped the case up in Exeter and I'm transferring back in four weeks."

"To Branden Bay?"

"Yes."

"At Christmas?"

He nodded. "I want us to be serious," he said in a low voice staring into my eyes. "These past weeks have taught me, I can't afford to lose you. The job will just have to work itself out." Then he kissed me in front of everyone.

I heard cheers from my friends but ignored them.

H pulled away and smiled at me with his dark eyes. "I love you, Becky James."

NOT ONLY IS CHRISTMAS COMING, but so are Becky's parents. Christmas has to be perfect. They will be meeting her boyfriend for the first time.

After she's roped into carol singing, a choir member is found dead with one on Becky's mince pies stuffed into their mouth.

Becky is soon haunted by the singing spirit and is kept awake at night by a far from tuneful voice.

Can Becky solve the mystery surrounding this untimely death, before her parents arrive home? Or will her plans for the perfect Christmas be ruined?

BUY the *Christmas in Branden Bay* novella

IF YOU WOULD LIKE to join my mailing list and be alerted of my new releases and receive a free digital copy of my novella about Becky's grandma Constance, then please visit www.kellymasonbooks.com

REVIEWS ARE REALLY helpful to an author so please leave one on Amazon or Goodreads if you have a few moments.

ACKNOWLEDGMENTS

I'd like to thank my creative writing tutor Rosemary Dun, both inside the OU and out! You encouraged me to pursue novel writing and gave me so much information and guidance, I'm still reading the handouts! You are amazing. Thanks also goes to my brilliant mentors Alison Knight and Jenny Kane of Imagine Creative Writing and their Novel in a Year course, which gave me lots of help and kept me on track. And Alison is also my editor - thanks for all you do xx

Thanks to the inspirational friends I met through the Romantic Novelists' Association, and the Bristol writing community (I'm too scared to list everyone in case I miss someone off!) And to my Beta readers Cinnomen Matthews McGuigan, Michelle Armitage, Shell Rice Mortimer and Leanne Goodall. Thanks also to Helen Blenkinsop who is a guru on the 'hook' and amazon ads. And thanks to my best writing friends – Callie Hill, Claire O'Conner and Jenny Treasure, for also being beta readers and for sharing the journey with me.

Thank you to my advance reader team who are

really supportive and there for me, even from the first book. And especially Carol Kurimbokus who picks up those last pesky typos. I really appreciate it.

Thank you to those on my mailing list who interact with me. And thanks to those who send me cake ideas: Val, Keith, Carolyn, David, Janice, Tanith, Pamela-Anne, Nancy, Carrie-Ann, Carol, Sylvia, Marion, Christie and Betty.

Thanks to Tracey Hadfield who always has a ghost hunting story to scare me with.

Thanks to my sassy cats, even though they boss me about on a daily basis.

Thanks to my family for supporting me and reading my books, especially Dad, Uncle Stephen and Debjita.

And finally, thanks to Gary for putting up with me tapping away at the keyboard 24/7.

Printed in Dunstable, United Kingdom

67319884R00153